MOHINDER'S WAR

MOHINDER'S WAR

BALI RAI

BLOOMSBURY EDUCATION
LONDON OXFORD NEW YORK NEW DELHI SYDNEY

BLOOMSBURY EDUCATION
Bloomsbury Publishing Plc
50 Bedford Square, London, WC1B 3DP, UK
29 Earlsfort Terrace, Dublin 2, Ireland

BLOOMSBURY, BLOOMSBURY EDUCATION and the Diana logo are trademarks of
Bloomsbury Publishing Plc

First published in Great Britain in 2020 by Bloomsbury Publishing Plc

A catalogue record for this book is available from the British Library

ISBN: PB: 978-1-4729-5837-2; ePDF; 978-1-4729-5838-9; ePub: 978-1-4729-5839-6

6 8 10 9 7 5

Typeset by Newgen KnowledgeWorks Pvt. Ltd., Chennai, India
Printed and bound by CPI Group (UK) Ltd., Croydon CR0 4YY

To find out more about our authors and books visit www.bloomsbury.com
and sign up for our newsletters

PROLOGUE

I pointed to the stranger.

'Who's that woman?'

Mum frowned.

'Which one?'

'The one in the light blue coat,' I said. 'She was crying all the way through the service.'

'Oh,' said Mum. 'She must be someone your great-grandfather knew years ago. I haven't seen her before.'

As we left the crematorium, I saw more unfamiliar mourners. Some were old, others younger, and there were some news reporters too. My great-grandfather had flown in World War

Two, as an Indian attached to the Royal Air Force. He had lived to be a hundred-and-five years old, and we had been close.

I was only thirteen, but we'd had loads in common, which might sound strange, but you never met my great-grandfather. Even at the end, he was like a kid – full of humour and always telling great stories. We both loved books, and when his eyesight failed, I would read to him whenever I could. My grandfather, his only son, had died before him, and he'd lost many of his friends during and after the war. Sometimes I'd sit with him in the gardens of his care home, and he'd become suddenly wistful. He'd stare sightlessly into the distance, as though he'd spotted some dear old friend, or been haunted by some dark memory.

Later, my home town held a gathering in his memory. I was standing by an open fire exit, keeping cool on a hot day, when the unfamiliar woman appeared by my side. Her hair was silvery-grey and her eyes a deep, dark brown. She had a mole on her right cheek and a gap between her front teeth.

'You must be Simpreet,' she said.

My confusion was obvious, and the woman smiled and quickly explained.

'Mohinder told me about you. In one of the last letters he sent me. He enclosed a photograph of you with your mother. I recognised your mother at the crematorium.'

'My great-grandad wrote to you?'

She nodded.

'Every week, until a few years ago. Then the letters stopped. I thought he had died, and my heart was broken, but then I saw a news item about him.'

'He went blind,' I told her. 'I guess he couldn't write any more. We were really close, so I used to read to him. But he never mentioned you.'

I was puzzled by her words. What did she mean by heartbroken, and why? Instead of concealing my thoughts, I asked her. The woman smiled.

'Forthright and fearless,' she said. 'Just like my brave Mo…'

'It sounds like you loved him.'

'I did,' she admitted. 'I still do. But not in the way most people might think.'

'So, how did you know him?'

The woman sighed. I saw the same wistfulness in her expression as I'd seen in my great-grandfather's.

'Mo saved my life,' she explained. 'When I was about your age.'

She pointed outdoors.

'Come,' she said. 'Let's find a bench to sit on. I've got a story to share with you…'

ONE

The sound of failing engines awakened me before dawn. They howled and clattered and thumped, and for a moment, I thought that I might be in danger. However, the wailing soon passed by, and then came the explosion. Maman ran into my room, her long brown hair as wild as her expression.

'Joelle!' she cried. 'Joelle!'

'I'm fine, Maman.'

'It has crashed,' she added. 'Did you hear?'

I sat up in bed, nodded and shivered. It was late November and uncommonly cold, much like the previous winter had been. My bedroom window was ill-fitting, iced over and draughty, and my nose ran. The climate matched the mood of my country, overrun by Germans and without hope of liberty. France, in 1941, was a shadow of itself, shivering under oppressive forces.

'Will they come here?' I asked, talking of the Germans.

'It is probable,' Maman told me. 'Those dogs will do as they please.'

She spat out her words, her contempt for our conquerors obvious. Everyone hated the Nazis, bar those who collaborated with them. They were the enemy, to be thwarted and resisted, as best we could. Maman and Papa went further still, engaging with the *Maquis* – those who would later be remembered as the Resistance. We sheltered them when required and helped them on their secretive missions. All of which meant danger and possibly death.

For myself, then only thirteen years on this Earth, the concepts of oppression and mortality should have been unfamiliar things. Like far-off countries and exotic foods, they should have remained the stuff of stories. But we were under occupation, and my age meant nothing. Childhood, in its purest form, was impossible. So, I embraced my new life, despite my fears. I did as I was asked, like a good little soldier might, and each time we frustrated the enemy, however slightly, I felt proud and worthy. Such was my life, then.

'Where is Papa?' I asked.

'He left a while ago,' Maman replied. 'To light the ovens.'

My parents were bakers, with a small *boulangerie* at the heart of our little town. Before the Germans came, business was good, and we lived a charmed life, even though we were never rich. Back then, our town was lively and the people mostly cheerful. Many would gather in the central square, drinking and eating on the long summer evenings, and singing songs. Even the cold dark nights before Christmas were full of merriment. It was idyllic. To a small child, the world seemed vibrant and wholesome, and so wonderfully warm and full of possibilities. Before they came.

Afterwards, everything stopped. The warmth dissipated, the vibrancy dulled, and the people grew fearful and depressed. Our bakery suffered as food shortages took hold, and rationing meant that everyone went without. Yet still Papa would rise each morning and light the ovens.

'One day the flour will be delivered,' he'd often tell me. 'The war will end, and liberty will return.'

'So, then, save your fuel,' I would say to him. 'Until you need it.'

Papa would shake his head.

'The ovens must never grow cold,' he explained. 'They are hope, Joelle, and we must always have hope. If the fires go out, we have let these animals win. And we will not let them win.'

'So, we must keep the fires burning?'

'Always,' he replied, with a distant expression, as though he were forlorn in some way. 'Always…'

Now, Maman urged me to sleep once more.

'I cannot,' I replied. 'I cannot sleep. Not when they might come, and we have…'

'SHHH!' Maman told me. 'Do not even mention them!'

Down in our cellar, behind a secret door known only to us, hid two people. Two resistors. To think that they, and we, might be discovered chilled my bones more than any ice could.

'It will be fine,' Maman told me. 'Chin up, as I used to say in England.'

Maman was English by birth, from a town called Gravesend in Kent. I had never visited England at that time, but Maman was always full of stories of her childhood and had taught me her language.

'What shall we do?' I asked her. 'If the Germans come?'

'Nothing,' she advised. 'We will do nothing but continue our daily routines. We will be polite and friendly and cause no trouble. They will not suspect a woman and child of anything.'

I nodded and pulled the covers around myself, praying that she was right.

The plane crashed beyond our little house, in fields that had been owned by Monsieur Deschamps until the Nazis shot him and his family for Resistance activity. Their bodies were taken to the town square and left by the fountain. A warning to us all. Grace Deschamps had been my friend, only two years older than me. A happy and gentle girl with a kind heart. Now, as I trudged down an icy lane, I wondered what had happened to the pilot. Whether he had been German or British, or some other nationality. And I thought of Grace and how we had played together in the very fields where the plane had crashed.

Some distance away, several Germans searched the area, while another stood atop an armoured vehicle looking through field glasses. I was not concerned about them spotting me. I was just a young girl, heading in the opposite direction, towards a stream that ran through woodland. The woods were my secret place, my escape. As I approached the bank of the stream, however, another German appeared from the trees to my left. He was young, no more than twenty years old, and he half-smiled at me.

'Have you seen a man here?' he asked in poor French.

'No,' I replied. 'I have not seen anyone.'

'Are you sure?'

'Yes, sir,' I told him, showing my best manners, just as Maman had suggested.

'You live nearby?'

I turned and pointed out our house, about half a mile back towards town.

'There,' I told him.

He wore a grey overcoat, grey trousers and black leather boots caked in dirt. A rifle hung around his right shoulder.

'Are your parents at home?'

'Just my maman,' I replied. 'Papa is in town.'

'Very well,' he told me. 'Run along!'

I nodded and bid him good morning. At the edge of the woods, I turned and saw the soldier heading towards my house.

'Please don't find them,' I whispered. 'Please don't hurt Maman.'

I followed the stream until I came to a clearing. I knew the woods well and found my usual rock and sat down. The stream widened here, and its edges were icy. The water was pure and clear, and I sat to think about my life and my future, as I always did. I longed for the day that France would be free, but that day seemed a long way off. A dream, impossible to reach.

A sudden rustling broke my thoughts. To my right, from a thicket of bushes dwarfed by several great oak trees, came a thin and ragged fox. Its bright carroty fur brought a welcome splash of colour.

'*Bonjour*, Monsieur Renard,' I said.

The fox looked up at me, cocked his head, then continued to forage. Thinking no more of it, I turned back to the stream. That was when I heard something moaning. Startled, I jumped up and took a step away.

'Hello?'

When no one replied, I assumed that a small animal might be in the bushes – perhaps a victim of the fox. Only, the moaning grew louder and more human, and that was when I knew.

I edged closer to the thicket, and saw only branches and leaves, but in an awkward formation. As though they had been cut, moved and replaced – perhaps as cover for…

'Hello?' I said again, only this time in English.

'Help…' someone croaked in reply. 'Please!'

The person was male, and English, but with an accent I had never heard. I had seen some Senegalese soldiers before the Germans took over – marching with French troops, speaking the language in strong accents, but this was different. It had to be the English pilot of the crashed plane.

'Stay there!' I said. 'The Germans are looking for you.'

I pushed aside branches and lifted some away, and there he was, bloodied and bruised, but not overly so. He lay on his side, legs drawn up, so that he might better hide himself. He was dark-skinned with a moustache and beard, and on his head sat a wrap made of royal-blue cloth. His honey-coloured eyes seemed to plead with me.

'Don't worry,' I whispered. 'I won't tell the Germans. Stay here and I'll get my mum.'

'RAF,' he croaked. 'Thank you.'

That was how I met him.

TWO

We left the pilot hidden until nightfall but took him some water and a little food, once the Germans had gone. The bread was dark and hard, and consisted of flour dust more than flour itself. Maman also made coffee and laced it with a little brandy, to help with any pain the pilot might have been suffering. He sat up and thanked us, in heavily accented English, but Maman shushed him.

'Stay quiet and reserve your energy,' she said in English. 'My husband will be along soon, and then we'll get you inside.'

Maman stayed with him but sent me home to await Papa. When my father arrived, I explained the situation, and he hurried out to the woods.

'Wait here,' he told me. 'If you see or hear any German vehicles approaching, you know what to do.'

We had several alarms in case the Nazis were spotted. During the day, I would ring a bell, mounted in our small garden. It was a child's toy and easily excused as a bit of fun but could be heard some distance away. We also closed the shutters in a specific way, just in case we couldn't reach the bell. If the upstairs windows were shuttered during the day, they signified danger. And after dark, we used flashlights, flicked on and off, to warn of peril. It was the latter that Papa left with me.

'Hurry, Papa!' I replied.

My parents returned half an hour later, with the pilot in tow. He was tall, towering over them both, and his beard was caked in dried blood. Papa helped him to sit at the kitchen table, and Maman began to boil some water.

'I'll clean up your wounds,' she explained in English. 'No serious injuries, by the look of you.'

The pilot nodded.

'I was lucky,' he replied. 'Managed to get out before the plane went down.'

'Perhaps not so lucky,' said Papa. 'This area is thick with Nazis.'

The man nodded and then looked at me.

'Thank you,' he said. 'I am Mohinder Singh. People call me Mo.'

'Joelle Breton,' I replied.

He smiled and sat back, rubbing his left shoulder.

'I think it was damaged during my fall,' he said. 'Hurts.'

Maman soaked some cloths in hot water, allowed them to cool a little, and began to clean Mo's face. Meanwhile, Papa finished the coffee and cut some more slices of stale bread, which he placed on a plate with a few slivers of cheese.

'We don't have much today,' he said in apology. 'I should have more food tomorrow.'

Mo shook his head.

'I cannot eat your food,' he told me. 'I will be fine until morning.'

'Nonsense!' said Maman. 'Eat, please.'

Eventually Mo relented. Once Maman had cleaned him up, he tucked in, and drank down his coffee. Afterwards, Papa poured some wine but again Mo was hesitant.

'I don't drink alcohol,' he told us.

Maman's face fell.

'Oh, I'm so sorry,' she said. 'I didn't realise. I put brandy in your coffee earlier.'

Mo shrugged.

'It is not a problem,' he said.

He gestured towards the glass.

'It smells very good,' he added.

Papa nodded.

'It's not the best,' he replied. 'But we cannot pick and choose these days.'

'Perhaps, then,' said Mo, 'I will try a little. I cannot afford to be picky in my current situation either.'

He took a sip and grimaced.

'It is bitter,' he said.

'An acquired taste,' said Papa, and the two of them laughed.

I was sitting on a stool, by the fireplace. The embers glowed and crackled and kept me warm on another chilly evening.

'Where are you from?' I asked.

Mo took another sip of wine and smiled.

'England,' he said. 'I am based just south of London.'

'But you're not English?'

Mo shook his head.

'I am from India,' he told me. 'From a place called Punjab.'

'Hush, Joelle,' Maman said in French. 'Leave the poor man be.'

Mo didn't speak any French, but he seemed to understand.

'It is fine,' he told Maman. 'Children should be curious. I come from a family of farmers. We are Sikhs, although…'

He looked at the wine glass.

'I am not a practising Sikh.'

I shrugged.

'I don't know what a Sikh is,' I admitted. 'Is that why you wrap cloth around your head.'

Mo laughed again.

'It's called a *pagri*,' he told me. 'And yes, that's why. Sikhism is a religion – from India.'

'*Pagri*,' I repeated, although not very well. 'I like it. Perhaps you should get one, Papa?'

My father grinned.

'I'm not sure it would suit me,' he replied.

'You would certainly look taller,' I joked.

Papa was short and stout, with sandy hair that was beginning to recede. Maman was slightly taller than Papa, and of a similar build, but her hair was dark brown to match her eyes, and she had a mole on her right cheek, just above the jawline – just like me. Compared to them, Mo was a giant – over six feet tall with strong hands and wide shoulders. His dirty uniform was either grey or blue – I cannot really remember. All I recall is that it grew dirtier with each passing day. But then, considering what we overcame, that is unsurprising.

A knock at the door broke our conversation.

'Quick, hide!' I whispered to Mo, but Maman shook her head.

'Don't worry, she said. 'It will be Beatrice. She said she would call by.'

Maman went to let her in, and when Beatrice saw Mo, her eyes grew wide.

'You are *English*?' she asked, her accent thick. 'The plane that crashed?'

'Yes,' said Mo.

'My God!' she replied. 'The Germans go crazy looking for you.'

She turned to my parents. She wore a navy dress under a long grey coat, with black ankle boots. The coat was oversized because she often smuggled food and other contraband within its lining. Today, she removed some sausage and a package of butter from it as she spoke, in French.

'Can you hide him, Nora?' she asked, placing her smuggled goods on our table.

'Of course,' said Maman.

'You understand the risks?' she asked, her pale blue eyes wide.

My parents nodded in unison.

'We do not care about risks,' Papa told her. 'Only that France might one day be free again.'

Beatrice nodded.

'Me also, Jacques,' she said. 'I will arrange for the ones hiding downstairs to move on. And I must speak to Claude at once!'

As she hurried back into the night, Mo looked at us.

'Who was that?' he asked.

'Beatrice?' I replied. 'She is *Maquis* – a rebel, like us.'

'And who is hidden downstairs?' he added.

I looked to Maman, and she shrugged.

'They are wanted by the Germans,' Maman explained. 'We often hide people, Mo. You'll be safe here.'

THREE

Mo seemed much better the next morning. He was sitting with Maman when I came downstairs.

'We've been talking about England,' Maman said in English.

'You miss your homeland,' I said.

'It's only natural,' Maman replied. 'But it's not my home, Joelle. That is here, with you and Jacques.'

'Home is about the people you love,' Mo added. 'It is where you feel loved.'

'Do you miss India?' I asked, hoping that my English sounded okay.

'Of course,' he said, 'but I miss England too. The people have been very kind since I arrived.'

'Why did you come?'

Mo shrugged, wincing as he did so.

'To help,' he said. 'The British rule my country, and we are subjects of His Majesty, the king. I felt it was my duty.'

I shrugged this time.

'We have no kings in France,' I told him. 'And I do not understand why anyone does.'

'Hush, Joelle!' said Maman. 'Mo is our guest. You will not interrogate him.'

'Please,' said Mo. 'I am happy to answer Joelle's questions.'

I sat and ate a breakfast of hard bread and cold sausage, with a little coffee from the pot. Papa had hidden a supply of coffee beans when the war started, but they were running out. Soon, only the chicory-laden muck that passed for coffee under the Occupation would remain. I had heard others complain about it, call it mud water and sewer juice. So, I savoured what we had left.

'Have you heard from Beatrice?' I asked in French.

Maman nodded.

'There's no need to keep this from Mo,' she replied in English. 'I have told him all about our work.'

'I am very heartened to hear of the Resistance,' Mo told me. 'In England, news of France is always dire. And with the Dunkirk evacuation and the German bombing campaign, there seems little to be happy about. I admire your bravery.'

'It is the least we can do,' I told him, parroting my papa. 'When I am older, I want to be proud of what I did in these times. To feel like I helped.'

'Such deep thoughts for someone so young,' said Mo. 'I despair at what this world has done to our children.'

Our children, that's what he said, with sincerity and passion. That was the first inkling I got of his moral character, his belief that all of humanity was one and the same. I would soon learn that he meant every word.

I went for a bicycle ride just after midday, as Papa returned with a bag of black-market goods. I was feeling trapped and in need of the outside world, as awful as that had become, and I wanted to check on someone dear to me.

'Extras,' said Papa, as we passed in the lane that led from our house, back towards town.

'Real bread?' I asked.

'I'm afraid not,' said Papa, dashing my hopes. 'I will try to get some soon, my love. I promise.'

'I'm going to see Mrs Moreau,' I told him. 'I won't be long.'

'Take these for her,' said Papa.

He took some bread and a package of butter from his bag and placed them in my bicycle's pannier.

'Make sure she accepts them,' he told me.

Mrs Moreau ran a tiny bookshop in town and I loved to read. She was in her late seventies and widowed, and she treated me like a lost grand-daughter. Her back was hunched now, and she moved slowly, wrapped in her dark shawl like a sickly blackbird. Her shop had closed for business when the Germans arrived, and very few people were allowed in. I was one of the exceptions, and when I knocked on the door, she peered through the dusty glass and smiled.

'*Chérie!*' she exclaimed, as she let me in. 'Oh, I have missed you. Where have you been?'

'I'm sorry,' I told her. 'I wanted to come sooner, but there was too much to do.'

Mrs Moreau pulled me into a hug.

'That other business?' she asked.

'Exactly,' I replied with a wink.

We walked through the dusty bookshop, past piles and piles of old books and several stuffed animals that Mr Moreau had collected when he was still alive. When I was younger, the animals had frightened me, but now I found them comforting – another reminder of our old lives.

'Excuse the mess, my dear,' said Mrs Moreau. 'I no longer have the energy to clean up. And I have not ventured upstairs since last summer.'

I could hear mice and somewhere I knew that Mrs Moreau's huge black cat, Roland, was stalking them, ready to pounce. No doubt he would bring us his latest catch, and purr with pride when he did.

'We'll sit in the kitchen,' said Mrs Moreau. 'Would you like something to eat?'

I shook my head.

'I'm fine,' I replied. 'I just wondered if you needed anything.'

Like most people, my parents often came by food and other necessities on the black market. Some of that food made its way into Mrs Moreau's hands. In return, she let me take books home and never asked for their return.

'What can an old lady need?' she said, just as she always did.

I took the bread and butter from my jacket and set them down. The kitchen was a mess, overflowing with unwashed dishes and littered with rubbish. I began to clear up, as Mrs Moreau fussed about me, telling me to leave things be.

'Please,' I insisted. 'You only need to ask. I can come and clean up more regularly.'

'You're very good to me,' she replied. 'Now, tell me what's been going on. Are we winning yet?'

On the way home, with two tattered but interesting books nestling in my bicycle basket, I wondered how Mrs Moreau would survive the Occupation. I worried for her, and often dreamed of moving her to our house. But she was a stubborn old goat and would not leave her bookshop until she was carried away in a coffin. The thought of it saddened and angered me. So, as I passed a German vehicle, I swore under my breath – a curse I had often heard my mother use, when she thought I was not listening.

At the edge of town, I turned down the lane that led home. A bell tinkled behind me, and Beatrice appeared at my side, riding her own bicycle. She wore the same clothes as the day before, and I wondered what she'd hidden in the folds of her coat.

'Good evening,' she said. 'Have you been bothering that old witch again?'

I smiled.

'Mrs Moreau is not a witch,' I replied. 'At least, not to me.'

'Oh, the stories I could tell you,' said Beatrice. 'You know she once said I had a face made for slapping?'

'Perhaps you upset her?' I suggested.

Beatrice smiled back.

'How is she holding up?'

'Not great,' I said. 'I will keep a closer eye on her.'

'You are a fine little soldier,' Beatrice told me. 'With children like you, we will survive this hell.'

At our door, we dismounted, and I noticed the horse and cart by the garden wall.

'Ah,' said Beatrice. 'Claude has arrived.'

FOUR

Maman was fussing when I entered the kitchen. The two men we'd been hiding were at the table, and Mo sat with them. The Resistance members were young – in their twenties. One was short and fair, the other taller with dark hair and an olive complexion. I had not spoken to them at all, nor seen them very much, even though they had been living in our cellar. Both had grown beards and I could smell their body odour from where I stood. Neither man spoke.

'You must take food,' Maman was saying. 'Who knows when you will eat again?'

'It is fine,' Claude told her.

Claude was Beatrice's brother – a local farmer with thick, calloused hands and a gruff temper. His nose was huge and bent, the result of a boxing match from his teenage years. Had I not known him, I would have taken him for a ruffian.

'We must get moving,' Claude told Maman.

'Some bread and butter, that's all,' said Maman.

'Very well,' said Claude. 'But hurry!'

Papa was sitting by the fireplace, drinking wine and chewing on a lump of bread.

'How was Mrs Moreau?' he asked me. 'Did you get some books?'

I nodded and set my latest treasures down beside him.

'Some ghost tales and a pirate adventure,' I replied. 'She is fine and thanks you for the rations.'

'I must go and see her,' said Papa. 'Are you hungry?'

I nodded.

'Nora,' said Papa. 'A plate for Joelle, *chérie*, and perhaps Beatrice too?'

Maman sliced some bread, buttered it, and poured me a little wine. She did the same for Beatrice.

'There is some cheese,' said Papa.

As Claude and the men left, Beatrice took a seat, and at first we ate in silence.

'The Germans have placed a reward on your capture,' Beatrice eventually informed Mo, via Maman's interpretation. 'We must think very carefully about our next move.'

'I need to return to England,' said Mo. 'Perhaps I could make my way north and find a fisherman willing to cross the Channel?'

Once Maman had translated, Beatrice's face lit up in alarm.

'No, no,' she said. 'It is too risky! The northern coast is teeming with German patrols, and the Channel is treacherous. Calais, Boulogne, Dunkirk – they are all out of bounds.'

'So, what then?' Mo asked, his face falling along with his expectations.

'South,' Beatrice replied. 'We have contacts in Toulouse. They can take you into the Basque region, and on to Santander. It will be safer to find passage there.'

'Into Spain?' said Papa. 'But won't that be just as risky?'

'No,' said Beatrice. 'We have many Spaniards fighting with us. They know the region well and have contacts of their own. Compared to the northern coast, Spain will be easy.'

She eyed Mo for a moment.

'Besides,' she eventually said. 'The people of the south are swarthier than those around here. With a haircut and shave, he will not look so conspicuous…'

Maman finished translating, and Mo's shoulders slumped.

'I do not wish to cut my hair,' he told us. 'My hair has never been cut. It is part of who I am.'

I looked up at him.

'But you will always stand out with it,' I told him. 'You will get caught.'

Mo shook his head.

'Then let me go,' he said. 'I would rather get caught.'

Maman sighed.

'Let's think about our options,' she said in English. 'We have some time.'

Only, we didn't.

The Germans came without warning, at around three in the morning. Mo had been sleeping in a spare bedroom, the third of three. When the Germans began to bang on the door, I shot out of bed and into my parents' room.

'Take him down to the cellar!' Papa told me. 'Now!'

I ran to fetch Mo and led him downstairs. We went through the kitchen to a larder and entered it. Inside, hidden behind some sacks of firewood, lay a secret panel. I set the shelves aside and pushed on the panel, uncovering stone steps that led down into the gloom. The cellar had been divided in two with a brick wall. One set of stairs was accessible from the front of the house, and the second set hidden from view.

'Come on!' I said, leading the way without any light to guide us. Once Mo had passed by, I repositioned the sacks and replaced the panel, pulling it tightly into place. The back of the panel had been densely padded with straw, so that it wouldn't sound too hollow if tapped.

'Keep quiet,' I whispered. 'They will not find us down here.'

The sound of boots and raised voices reached us, and then I heard a shout and Maman screamed. My heart thumped in my chest and I held back a scream of my own.

'Dear God!' I said. 'Please don't let them hurt her!'

Suddenly, I heard a banging noise, followed quickly by a second and third. I guessed that the Germans were using their rifle butts to check the walls and floor of the house, to find any secret compartments.

'How can they know?' I whispered to Mo.

'I'm not sure,' he replied. 'I am sorry to cause you so much danger.'

'Don't be sorry,' I told him. 'It's not like we were safe before you appeared.'

We stayed hidden for over an hour, as the Germans searched every inch of the house. They were careless in their search, and I heard them breaking dishes and splintering wood. Eventually, though, they relented and left. Finally, I heard the panel being removed and my mother's whispered voice call out.

We ascended the steps to find the house a mess, and Papa nursing a bloodied lip.

'What have they done?' I wailed, tears filling my eyes.

'It's nothing,' said Papa. 'Just an over-zealous German. I'll live.'

Mo's head dropped, and he apologised once again.

'This is not right,' he told us. 'I will leave and remove you from danger.'

Maman took his hand.

'No,' she told him, her tone stern. 'This is what we live through, all of us. They killed our friends, our neighbours. They took our Jewish folk away, for God knows what reason. They have stolen our country and our liberty. We must stand against them, don't you see? If we can save you, you might one day return and save us from them. We *must* help you.'

'But you have a child, a home, a life…' he replied.

'I have a child and a home, yes,' said Maman. 'But this is not life. This is not a life at all.'

Mo looked at me and I saw a tear fall from his left eye. He wiped it away and sat down and watched silently as I tended to Papa.

FIVE

Over the next few days, Mo and I began to share stories. Mostly, it was I who asked the questions and Mo was generous in his responses. He seemed to enjoy spending time with me and I wondered if he had any children. When I asked, he simply shrugged.

'I am not married,' he replied.

'You have a sweetheart, then?' I said. 'In India?'

Mo grinned.

'In my culture, such things are frowned upon,' he told me. 'There *was* a girl, but her father thought me an unsuitable match, and so I came to England unwed.'

'Do you write to her?'

'Yes, but in secret,' he revealed. 'Her father would not approve, so we pretend that the letters are from a female friend.'

'But that is silly!' I replied. 'Surely her father can see that you are brave and worthy?'

Mo shook his head.

'Not that man,' he told me. 'He would rather she married a rich boy than some pilot thousands of miles from home.'

He had removed his *pagri* and his long hair was tied atop his head, in a bun. This was unheard of for French men, and I found it amusing and then intriguing.

'Have you really never cut your hair?' I asked.

'Never,' he replied. 'Sikhs are forbidden from cutting their hair, or shaving. I trim my beard, but that is all.'

'Why is that?' I asked.

He talked of someone called *Nanak Dev-Ji* and told how he was a rich man who gave up his possessions to roam India. To help those in need.

'The religion began with him,' Mo told me. 'He is our first *guru*.'

'What is a *guru*?'

'The best translation is *teacher*,' Mo told me. '*Guru Nanak* taught the people that we are all one humanity, one people.'

'I think I like this man,' I replied with a smile. 'That is what I believe too.'

'You and your parents are Christians?' Mo asked.

'Maman is,' I told him. 'Papa and I are not so sure…'

'You do not believe in God?' he added.

I shrugged.

'Since the Germans came,' I said, 'I am not sure what I believe in. Only freedom and winning back my country.'

'You are too young to be part of this,' he replied.

I nodded.

'Perhaps,' I said. 'But what choice do we have?'

I told him about Grace and her family, and what the Nazis had done to them. When I was finished, Mo shook his head in sorrow.

'What could possess men so?' he asked. 'To kill children and women, and innocents?'

'Now do you see?' I asked. 'Why I am not sure about God and such things?'

'I do,' he replied. 'Just don't lose hope, Joelle. Without that, we are nothing.'

On his fifth day with us, after he had left the cellar where he now slept, washed and eaten a breakfast of bread and cheese, I took Mo outside. I was careful, making sure that no one was around to spot us, but Mo was uncertain.

'If someone sees us, you will get into trouble,' he told me.

Maman and Papa had gone to run errands and find more food. I knew that they would disapprove but Mo had been locked in our cellar. He needed the fresh air.

'I've checked twice,' I told him. 'There is no one within sight.'

Our house sat on the edge of town, some distance from the next dwelling. Behind us were poor Monsieur Deschamps' fields, the stream and woodland. The only way to access our house was the single-track lane. If anyone approached, we would see them coming.

'But there is too much risk.'

'Look at you,' I said. 'Your cheeks are sunken and your eyes red. You need to get some air. Besides, I have a secret place to show you.'

'Your clearing?'

I nodded. I had forgotten that I'd found Mo there.

'Not so secret, of course, but still…'

Mo shrugged.

'How far is the crash site?' he asked.

'Nearby,' I told him. 'Why?'

'I want to see if my things are still there,' he told me. 'If we could do that, then I'm happy to venture out.'

'What *things* do you mean?'

'A memento from my mother,' he told me. 'In my kit bag.'

'That will be more dangerous than going into the woods,' I pointed out.

'That is my wish,' he replied.

I nodded.

'We must be quick, though,' I told him. 'Maman will be cross if she returns to find us gone.'

'Not Papa?'

I grinned.

'Papa is soft,' I replied. 'It's Maman's temper you have to watch!'

I checked the lane again, just to be sure, and then we left via the garden and cut across a fallow and muddy field behind it. At the stream, we crossed a rickety footbridge, and then turned right, away from the woods. The crash site lay beyond the next field, through a thicket of oaks and maples. It did not take us long to reach it, and luckily, we found no Germans guarding the plane.

'Be quick!' I told Mo.

The plane was broken in half, and the engine had exploded. The ground around the wreckage was charred and debris lay all around us – bits of wing and fuselage and the propeller too. A section of the wing lay upside down, so that the red, white and blue RAF roundel was visible. Mo rummaged around the remains of the cockpit, until he found a grey canvas bag.

'It's here!' he exclaimed with a huge smile.

He opened it, discarding everything until he found a length of royal-blue cloth.

'What is that?' I asked.

'Another *pagri*,' he explained. 'My mother sent me away with it.'

He unravelled the cloth to find a wooden-beaded bracelet.

'This is a prayer string,' he said. 'You move the beads as you recite the words.'

I nodded.

'We call them rosaries,' I told him. 'Maman has many. This is all you came for?'

He nodded.

'The radio is destroyed, and there is nothing else of value, save some tools,' he explained.

He salvaged what he could, placing everything in his bag. When he was done, we turned back, and he thanked me for bringing him to the plane.

'Don't thank me yet,' I told him. 'We have not made it home.'

Back at the stream, I led the way towards my clearing. On arrival, we sat on the steep bank and Mo took out his rosary once more. The ground was damp but not too uncomfortable, and across the stream, a rabbit foraged amongst some bushes. I wondered if the fox was close by, watching and waiting.

'My mother is a devout Sikh,' Mo told me. 'I am not so religious, but this rosary carries her blessing. It is my only reminder of her. It is precious.'

I asked how the rosary was used, and he began to recite a prayer in his Punjabi language. I did not understand a word, and was about to ask, when I heard their voices.

'SHHHH!!!!' I whispered in alarm. 'GERMANS!'

SIX

We hurried into the bushes, close to where Mo had hidden after his crash. The plants were dense here, and we managed to find cover just before the German soldiers appeared. They trampled across the clearing in their dirty, heavy boots, guns at the ready and conversing in their own language. There were three in total, and they seemed to be exchanging jokes. Every so often, they would burst into laughter, and I grew angry at their arrogance. Here they were, occupying a foreign country with violence, and yet they seemed unconcerned. Happy, even.

'Do not move a muscle,' Mo whispered, as they closed in.

I got a sudden urge to pee, and squirmed. Mo sensed my discomfort, placing his hand on mine.

'Take courage,' he whispered.

They gave the bushes a cursory search but seemed uninterested in going any further. Thankfully, we had hidden deep enough not to be discovered. One of the Germans said something that made the others giggle like children.

'Dogs!' I whispered.

Something else caught their attention, a rustling from the far bank. The fox dashed from cover, a rabbit between its jaws. The soldiers were startled and one of them opened fire with a machine gun. The fox howled, and I covered my mouth, so they would not hear me cry out.

'SHH!' Mo warned, as the nearest soldier turned back towards us.

'Who is there?" he said in faltering French. 'Come out!'

My insides churned with fear. How could I have been so stupid? Now they would find us for sure.

The soldier began to hack at the foliage again, and we were seconds from being discovered. Mo edged further into the bushes, pulling me with him. However, our actions were pointless. Under my breath, I told my parents that I was sorry and that I loved them. Then I closed my eyes, awaiting our doom.

'Hans!' I heard another soldier shout.

They conversed in German before leaving in haste. I don't know what happened that day, but I am grateful. Had the soldier searched a moment longer, I would not have lived to tell this tale.

Later, after remaining hidden for some time, we emerged from the bushes and made our way back. We were extra cautious this time, wary of meeting any more Germans, but made it home without incident. Maman was waiting by the door and scolded me in French.

'Please,' Mo insisted. 'This was as much my fault. Blame me.'

'No,' said Maman. 'You do not know the area, nor the dangers we face each day. Joelle does and should know better.'

'But she is only a child,' said Mo.

'It matters little,' Maman told him. 'These are no ordinary times. There is no room for childishness, nor mistakes. Not when our very lives are at risk.'

I searched Mo's face with my eyes, hoping that he wouldn't mention our close call with the Nazis. Mo seemed to understand and gave a slight nod.

'Well, I am sorry anyway,' he told Maman. 'I put your child's life in danger and I must accept my responsibility. It will not happen again.'

Maman seemed taken by his manner and his words, and her features softened.

'Oh well,' she said. 'No harm done.'

I sighed in relief as she led us indoors.

That evening, Beatrice returned with a stranger in tow. The man seemed stern and unhappy and spoke in a gruff manner. Something about him caused me to be wary. His name was Vincent.

'The British pilot is ours,' he told Beatrice and Maman.

'Ours?' asked Maman.

'Yes,' Vincent insisted. 'We are the leaders of the Resistance here. We must decide what becomes of him.'

'But we can hide him quite easily,' Maman replied. 'He is not the first to see our cellar. He will not be the last.'

Mo wasn't with us. He was taking a bath, and I was glad that he could not hear. I wondered what he might make of being referred to as a possession.

'The British left us to rot,' Vincent told us. 'After their shameful retreat at Dunkirk, we paid the price. Now, in exchange for their pilot, they must pay too.'

'Are you *insane*?' snapped Maman. 'No one is using Mo as a bargaining chip!'

'Nora, please!' said Beatrice. 'This is for the good of France.'

'I am not insane,' Vincent growled. 'In return for their Indian, we will demand aid and weapons, and anything else we desire. The British claim to be our allies, but look how we suffer…'

I hated Vincent immediately. Some say that hate is too strong an emotion, but I don't care. I know what I felt, and even though I was a child, I understood clearly the depth of my feelings.

'We will take him in two days' time,' Vincent declared.

'Where will he go?' asked Maman.

'That is none of your concern,' he replied. 'We all have our roles to play. Yours is to help us and keep your nose from everything else. We know that you smuggle food and other goods. We allow that to happen. Be thankful and do not concern yourself with things that you can't understand.'

'So, what are *we*?' asked Maman, growing angry. 'Your servants?'

'No, but I *am* a leader,' Vincent told her. 'You have your duty. I have mine. They are not the same thing, however.'

'And if we refuse?' she added.

'Then you will be known as collaborators,' Vincent replied. 'The lowest of all.'

Maman turned to Beatrice.

'Get this man out of my house immediately,' she snapped. 'And do not ever bring him here again.'

She was livid, her face coloured, her eyes blazing.

'You come to my house and speak to me this way?' she asked him. 'Get out! And be thankful my husband is not here.'

Vincent shrugged and left, leaving Beatrice to apologise to Maman.

'He is a good man,' said Beatrice. 'Just a little blunt with his words. We must obey him.'

'He is a donkey's backside!' said Maman. 'And I obey no man with such arrogance.'

'You must agree,' said Beatrice. 'We have to get Mo away from here!'

'To be used as a bargaining chip by that man?' asked Maman. 'Never!'

Beatrice promised to return the following evening, then rushed out after Vincent. Maman slammed the door behind them, just as Mo appeared, his long hair hanging loose.

'What did I miss?' he asked.

Maman shook her head.

'I'll explain later,' she replied.

SEVEN

The following morning, I was given a supply run, and happily accepted it as always. This involved taking my bicycle and riding out into the countryside to meet a local farmer, Monsieur Garand. The farmer was another ally, and gave us eggs and milk, and sometimes meat too. Such things were classed as black market, available only by ration, but that did not stop us. The dangers were obvious, but I had never been searched. My age meant that the German patrols left me alone. Mostly they would smile and usher me on my way. I would be polite in return while cursing them under my breath. It was like a game, only with deadly consequences for losing.

'Joelle!' Monsieur Garand bellowed when he saw me. 'Oh my – what a pretty smile!'

'*Bonjour!*' I said, pulling up beside his cart.

We were three miles out of town, at the edge of some woodland, on a dirt track that only locals knew of. Monsieur Garand gestured at his cart.

'I have eggs,' he told me. 'And a surprise for you and your parents.'

'A surprise?'

Monsieur Garand winked and produced two skinned and gutted rabbits from his huge overcoat.

'I caught several yesterday,' he told me. 'They're still lovely and fresh!'

'Oh, I cannot accept them,' I began to say.

'Nonsense!' he replied. 'I insist that you do. When was the last time you tasted rabbit?'

I shrugged.

'Before the Germans,' I told him.

He spat in disgust.

'May God curse these insufferable devils!' he said.

He wiped a tear from his eyes, his hands thick with grime.

'Poor Henri Deschamps,' he added, speaking of my former neighbour. 'He was my friend. I cannot abide what they did to him and his beautiful family.'

I nodded and placed my hand on his forearm.

'One day we will be victorious,' I said.

'Yes, yes!' he replied. '*Vive la France!*'

Monsieur Garand had fought in the Great War, and he saluted. As always, I returned his salute, and that cheered him up.

'Ah, my little soldier!' he said with a grin. 'Now, for the rabbits, I have some onions and some carrots, and a little garlic also.'

He handed me the animals and produced another little package. I placed everything in the basket of my bicycle, underneath some books and a roll of hessian.

'And the eggs,' he said.

On the rear of my bicycle were two boxes or panniers, one each side of the wheel. We placed the eggs at the bottom, covering them with straw and some rotten onions that Monsieur Garand had kept especially. If I got stopped, the soldiers would see the blackened and weeping onions and not look any further. At least, that was our hope.

'Is your family well?' I asked.

'So, so,' he replied. 'And yours?'

'The same,' I told him. 'I'd better get going.'

'Come back soon,' said Monsieur Garand, 'and tell your papa that I have some brandy waiting for him!'

'I will,' I replied, setting off for home.

I did not get far before I spotted the Germans. They had blocked the road into town and were stopping everyone that passed. My heart thumped louder in my chest. My forehead began to sweat.

'No!' I whispered to myself.

There was another route, through the fields and around the checkpoint, but the ground was rutted and uneven, and my bicycle would not make it. I also had the option to ditch my contraband, but that wouldn't be ideal either. I stopped, dismounted, and pretended to check my bicycle's chain. All the while, I was watching the checkpoint, to see what they were searching for. One or two Germans searched people's bags and belongings, but most were simply asking them questions. I guessed that they were still hunting for Mo, and with my courage replenished, I set off again.

'You're just a schoolgirl, trying to get home,' I told myself, over and over again. 'They will not stop a little girl.'

As I drew towards the checkpoint, a young, dark-haired solider held up his hand. He spoke in broken and poor French.

'Please stop,' he told me. 'Where are you going?'

I pointed into town.

'My house,' I replied. 'I live on the far side, sir.'

The German soldier nodded.

'And what do you carry?'

I shook my head, trying to avoid his gaze and thinking furiously about what I would say next. I could not let him find my smuggled goods.

'Well?' he asked, as an idea took shape in my head. I would call his bluff and see if he wanted to touch some rotten vegetables.

'Just some books and some old onions,' I told him, hoping that my plan would work.

'Onions?'

I nodded.

'I found them by the roadside,' I lied. 'Please, sir, Maman can make soup with them.'

'Show me,' he said.

I got off and opened both panniers, and the stench rose from them immediately. The German swore in his own language.

'Enough!' he said in French. 'That's disgusting!'

I shrugged.

'We might be able to rescue one or two,' I said. 'Enough to eat, perhaps…'

He waved me away, shaking his head, and called me a pitiful creature. I waited until I was clear before grinning, satisfied and proud that I had fooled him.

Maman was delighted with the rabbits. As Mo and I watched on, she cut them up, and then set about making a stew. I thought of the fox in the clearing, wondered whether it had survived being shot. We were far more fortunate, I thought. Poor Monsieur Renard.

'I have never eaten rabbit,' Mo told us. 'Is this normal here in France?'

I grinned.

'It used to be,' I told him. 'Now, we have to beg, borrow or steal any meat.'

'Perhaps I could eat just the vegetables?' he said.

'You could,' I told him. 'But you'll miss out on the best bit. Rabbit is delicious.'

Maman cooked the onions in butter and a little flour, before adding carrots and some wine that was lying around.

'You should use better wine for such magnificent creatures,' she said. 'But we don't have any.'

Mo looked fascinated.

'This is how my mother makes chicken,' he told us. 'But we use ginger and spices too. And we don't add any wine.'

'Perhaps we might visit your country one day?' I said. 'I would like that very much.'

Mo nodded, and for a moment he was lost in thought.

'My region is very fertile,' he told me. 'The food is delicious, and the people are warm. You would be very welcome.'

As we waited for the stew to cook, we exchanged stories and Mo told us some more about the Punjab. He spoke of missing his mother's cooking and the games he loved to play as a child, and of his village and the people he knew.

The stew took two hours, and just as it was ready, Papa returned. I knew immediately that something was wrong.

'Papa?' I asked. 'What is it?'

He shook his head.

'It's Claude and the two men we hid,' he told us sorrowfully. 'They were captured.'

'Oh no!' said Maman. 'Do we know where they were taken?'

Papa shook his head once more.

'They were not taken anywhere, my love,' he explained. 'The Germans murdered them…'

EIGHT

I awoke deflated and depressed the following morning. The world felt colder, harsher, and less hopeful than ever before. As always, Papa had gone to the bakery before starting his errands. Maman was drinking coffee, having just let Mo out of the cellar. Our house guest seemed as dejected as I was. He sat next to Maman, his *pagri* removed, his beard overgrown, and his eyes sore.

'Joelle,' said Maman. 'Would you like breakfast?'

I shook my head and sat beside Mo.

'I don't feel very hungry this morning,' I told her. 'I don't feel much of anything.'

'The murders?' said Maman.

'Yes.'

Mo shifted in his seat, before sipping his coffee. He had eaten bread and butter, and a few slivers of cheese.

'I will leave,' he told us. 'I cannot thank you enough for protecting me, but I must go. Your lives are at risk while I stay.'

'No,' said Maman. 'You don't have to leave.'

'What about Vincent?' Mo asked, making clear that Maman had been honest with him.

Maman sighed.

'Vincent is not our concern,' she told him. 'You cannot allow yourself to be used by such men. We will find another way to get you back to England.'

'There is no other way,' Mo told her.

'Beatrice will help,' she said. 'After she has…'

I thought of Claude and his bent nose. His smelly clothes and gruff but warm laughter. Lying in a ditch somewhere, with a callous Nazi standing over him. How would Beatrice cope with losing her brother, I wondered. They were the last of their family, with no children, nor spouses. Now Beatrice was left all alone, and my heart ached for her. I had known them my entire life. Had stayed with them before the Germans came, played games with them, eaten with them. First Grace, now Claude. My heart was broken all over again.

I left Maman and Mo to talk and went to wash and get dressed. I needed fresh air. I needed my no-longer-so-secret place. Only, I did not get the chance. Beatrice arrived in a dreadful state, worn out from a night of tears and despair. When Maman let her in, she collapsed and sobbed, holding on to Maman's olive skirts.

'CLAUDE!' she groaned. 'MY BROTHER!'

Maman helped her to her feet, ordered me to fetch the brandy, and sat her down beside Mo. The alcohol was hidden in a barrel, and I found a new bottle. It was dusty and cobwebbed, but the liquid inside would calm Beatrice. Act as an anaesthetic even, to help her forget for just a while.

'Why?' Beatrice repeated over and over again. 'Why did they shoot him? Where is the justice, Nora? Where is the humanity?'

Her dark hair was a mess and her face patchy with a rash. I tapped Mo on the shoulder and nodded towards the kitchen door. He seemed anxious and guilt-ridden.

'Come on,' I said. 'Maman will deal with this.'

Outside, behind the garden walls, Mo seemed to relax. He sat on a wooden bench that Papa had made.

'I need a cigarette,' he said.

'I do not smoke,' I told him. 'It is a filthy habit!'

'Me neither,' he admitted. 'But isn't that what you do – smoke and drink in times of stress?'

I shook my head.

'The brandy will soothe her nerves,' I told him. 'In small measures, it is even medicine, perhaps. But how will stinking of an ashtray make you feel less stressed?'

Mo smiled. Actually, it was not quite a smile. It was the beginning of one, that suddenly disappeared when he remembered the situation.

'Are you feeling sad?' he asked.

I nodded. I had spent the night thinking first of Claude, and then Grace too. I'd also imagined losing my parents to such evil, and it had punctured a hole in my heart more agonising than any bullet might.

'I don't want my parents to die,' I admitted. 'The pain would be unbearable. I cannot explain how much I love them.'

'Then do not try to explain,' Mo told me. 'The inexplicability of your love is what makes it so true. It isn't something to be measured, Joelle. It is too instinctive to measure.'

I considered his words and found myself agreeing with him.

'You are very wise,' I told him. 'For someone so young...'

'I am twenty-six years of age,' he revealed. 'Old enough.'

'Is this how love is described in your faith?' I added. 'Is this what Sikhs are taught?'

Mo grinned.

'No,' he said. 'This is what all fortunate humans learn. Where they live, to whom they pray – none of that matters.'

'My parents are the kindest, finest and most decent human beings,' I said. 'I am fortunate to have them.'

'That is why you must let me leave,' he replied. 'You can see out the war here. Remain hopeful of a better future. If you resist, you put yourselves at risk.'

'And if we do not resist?' I asked. 'What then is the point of us? To live like sheep to be branded? To cower before bullies? Never!'

I hadn't realised the strength of my emotions, nor the volume at which I expressed them. Mo seemed taken aback, and I apologised at one, placing my pale hand upon his dark one.

'You are also one of the best humans I have met,' I told him.

'But I have only been here for a week,' he pointed out.

'A week, a day?' I said. 'Who cares, when it is so obvious?'

'Tell your parents you love them,' he advised. 'Trust me, they will never tire of hearing it.'

Maman came out, to ask after the raised voices.

'Nothing, Maman,' I replied. 'I was merely being passionate about my feelings.'

'Are you sure?' she asked.

I smiled at Mo, and then at her.

'I love you, Maman!' I said, and at once her face lit up. 'I love you as I love the sunshine and the snow, and Mrs Moreau's books and rabbit stew. And more, Maman – much more!'

I hugged her close and took in her scent and felt instantly better.

'I love you too,' she told me.

That evening, after darkness had fallen and we'd eaten our supper, Maman allowed Mo and me to take a walk.

'It's dark, Maman,' I said. 'We'll be perfectly safe.'

'Just be careful,' she told us. 'You hide at the first sign of trouble, understand?'

Mo swore that he would protect me.

'You have my oath,' he told Maman. 'I will not let Joelle come to any harm.'

Maman smiled and gave me a little hug. If only I had known. If only, somehow, I had seen my future. If only I had stayed at home…

We were walking back from the woods, lighting the way with a rusty oil lamp. The air was cold and crisp, and my nose ran. It felt like a perfect winter's night, and Mo was busy telling me about his childhood, and his younger siblings. He had retied his turban and looked like a prince in the lamp's golden glow. His dark eyes shone.

We approached the garden from the fields, my house in front of us.

'Wait!' Mo suddenly growled, pulling me down so that we were hidden by the wall.

'What is it?'

'Something is wrong,' he whispered.

My stomach somersaulted with fear.

'Why do you say that?'

His expression was serious, his brow furrowed.

'The door has been kicked in,' he revealed.

'What?' I exclaimed as I shot up.

'Joelle, no!' he insisted, pulling me down again. 'Wait!'

'But what about Maman and Papa?' I begged. 'We must check on them!'

Mo nodded but did not move for a moment. It was the correct decision. Suddenly, we heard loud voices. Maman and Papa, and then some Germans. They seemed to be arguing and then Maman screamed. I held in my own cry, fearful of being discovered. Doing what my parents had always taught me.

Run, hide, but whatever you do, *don't* get caught.

'Liars!' I heard a German soldier shout. 'We know who you are!'

I heard Papa protesting innocence and then a thud as Maman screamed again. More shouting followed, and Mo began to pull me away.

'Run!' he whispered. 'Back to the trees, Joelle. Run and hide, and I will try to save them…'

Never mind think, I could barely breathe. My chest grew tight and my legs felt hollow and full of nothing but air. I stumbled to my feet and did as Mo said. And as I ran, I sobbed and sobbed, so great was my terror. Not my parents, I begged. Not my parents…

And then the shooting began…

NINE

I stopped running and turned, and the air around me seemed to buzz and grow heavy on my shoulders. My heart beat so fast, I thought it might explode. I remember screaming, but there was no sound. Like some dumb animal, I stood and wailed, and could not move. Mo appeared before me. He scooped me into his arms and carried me back towards the trees. Once past the treeline, he kept on going, bullying his way through thick undergrowth as though it were nothing. I did not stop screaming until we reached my clearing, and there I grew limp and the light in my eyes began to fade.

I know that I passed out. I know because Mo shook me to my senses and covered my mouth with his hands.

'Dogs!' he said, pulling me further into the woods. Further away from my parents.

As I heard the animals bark, we followed the stream.

'We must try and throw them off our scent,' he told me. 'Maybe if we run in the water?'

He took my hand again, and we jumped into the icy stream. The freezing water came as a jolt, and I was instantly fully conscious and aware.

'Keep running!' Mo told me.

We splashed on until the stream widened before climbing the opposite bank. Behind us, the dogs drew nearer, and I heard more German soldiers.

'There!' said Mo.

He pointed at a huge oak tree, and behind it, a narrow path probably used by hunters.

'Where does that lead?' he asked.

Only I had never ventured so deeply into the woods.

'I have no idea,' I told him.

'It doesn't matter,' he replied. 'We have no choice.'

Some fifty yards down the path grew wider. We ran into a small lane, lined by tall hedgerows on either side. Further along there was a house sitting in darkness.

'Come on!' said Mo.

'I know that house. It is deserted!' I told him. 'I didn't realise it could be reached through the woods.'

We sprinted down the lane, though the overgrown front garden, and past a rotten wooden door, Inside, the house had been left to ruin, and I heard rodents scurry away. A small parlour led into a larger kitchen area, and at the rear were stone stairs, similar to my own house. But the upper storey had collapsed, and the stairwell was impassable.

'Where now?' I asked.

Mo was sweating profusely, his turban darker where it sat on his forehead.

'Maybe there is an outbuilding?' he wondered aloud.

We raced into the yard, and in the distance, I heard the dogs barking once more. The Germans had found the lane, and soon they would find us. We were running out of time.

Mo had stopped by an old well. He was examining a rope, which had once held a pail. Suddenly, he pulled the rope free and drew it up. It was very long, probably twenty feet in total, and he began to tie thick knots along its length.

'Is there any more rope anywhere?' he asked.

My eyes had grown used to the dark by now, and I managed to search the area around us. I found a rusting shovel, a pitchfork, and some wooden crates, but nothing else.

'No rope!' I said, as the dogs closed in.

Mo picked up a rock and dropped it down the well, counting until he heard a splash.

'Ten,' he said. 'That is a long way down!'

He reconnected the rope, via a pulley wheel and made sure it was tight.

'Trust me,' he said. 'And do exactly as I say.'

Before I could react, he took hold of the rope, clambered over the side of the well and began to descend using the knots as footholds. The rope swung precariously and creaked under his weight but held fast. He held out his right hand.

'Come on!' he whispered. 'Climb over and hold on to me.'

'But what if we fall?' I said, hesitating.

'Joelle!' he urged. 'The Germans will be here any second. I promise you won't fall.'

He did not convince me. The barking of German shepherd attack dogs did. I leaped over to him but was too hasty. The rope swung and groaned, and I thought it would snap. Mo did not wait. As the dogs entered the yard, he began to climb down the knots. I clung on to him for dear life, his beard tickling my face.

'Do not make a single sound,' he whispered, once we'd come to a stop.

Above us, the dogs growled and snarled, but their masters paid them no heed. I heard the soldiers curse and swear, but they did not look down the well. We hung there for a long time, as they searched every inch of the abandoned farmhouse. My feet were resting on Mo's, my arms around his shoulders. I worried that Mo's grip might loosen. But he held fast and did not show an ounce of fatigue. However, my arms began to tire, and quickly.

'I cannot hold on much longer,' I whispered.

'You must!' he replied. 'We cannot die here, Joelle. Not now!'

I took a deep breath and willed myself greater strength. It was painful and scary, and I knew that I might let go at any second.

'They're leaving,' Mo whispered eventually.

Sure enough, the sound of barking dogs and cursing Germans receded. Only when he was absolutely certain, did Mo begin to ascend. He carried both of us with ease, and soon I was climbing out of the well.

'My parents!' I said.

Mo nodded, then lowered his head.

We found cover in the farmhouse's barn and sheltered there until dawn. Mo told me to rest, but I could not. Neither could he.

'I want to go to my parents,' I said, over and over again.

Only, deep inside, I knew that it was too dangerous. We needed to wait until there was no more threat. However, we had no idea what awaited us at my house. How would we know that danger had passed?

'Just try to rest,' Mo told me, as I held his hand and hoped for the best. Trouble was, hope was hard to find in those circumstances.

When, finally, we emerged, our trek back was slow and cautious. The closer we got to my house, the more my dread increased. The veins in my neck pulsed with tension and my legs wobbled. As we drew near, Mo told me to wait.

'We need to be sure,' he told me. 'And then I will go first.'

'No!' I insisted. 'They are my parents. I will go…'

'I cannot allow that,' Mo told me. 'I cannot let you face danger before me. That is not possible, Joelle.'

I knew that he was protecting me. I knew that he did not want me to discover some grisly scene. But truth be told, I already knew what we might find. And even though I told myself that I could handle it, I was not ready…

TEN

Maman was slumped across the kitchen table. She seemed to be asleep. Papa was splayed across the stone floor. I will not describe much more, because it feels wrong somehow. It feels mechanical and inhuman, precisely the opposite of what my parents actually were. In the long time since their murders, I have tried to forget the scene in the farmhouse that morning. Instead, I remember their warmth and their smiles, and the unconditional love they had for me.

I did not scream when I saw them. I did not moan or cry or fall about in grief. Perhaps Mo's presence helped me, I cannot be sure. But I was very glad to have his support.

'Come away, Joelle,' he whispered. 'There is nothing to be done.'

I ignored him a moment, taking in the scene and wiping away a few tears. Then I turned, and we walked back into the garden. The lane was quiet now, and no one approached from town. I saw no German soldiers and heard no attack dogs. The morning on which everything changed, and my old existence ended, seemed just a normal winter's morning.

'We must bury them,' I said to Mo. 'They cannot stay there. Not like that.'

'If we bury them,' Mo replied, 'the Germans will know we've been back. It might endanger us further.'

'What danger is left to us?' I asked him. 'Death? I no longer care about that. My parents are gone, and I am all alone.'

Mo shook his head.

'Not alone,' he told me. 'I swore that I would protect you, Joelle. Now that oath is stained in blood, and I will never forget it. Your parents saved me. In return, they lost their lives. Now you are my responsibility. If you are willing, I will take care of you.'

I nodded, wiping away more tears. Mo put his arms around me and pulled me closer.

'Cry, Joelle,' he told me. 'Do not hold these feelings inside. You must let your emotions breathe.'

Only then did I sob, and as Mo embraced me, I heard a bicycle approaching. I gave a start and looked up, but Mo told me not to panic.

'It is Beatrice,' he said.

She dismounted by the garden wall and walked through the gates. Her face fell when she saw us. She wore black garments, in mourning for her brother. They were very apt.

'Please, no!' she said in French.

'Maman and Papa are dead,' I told her, my tone blank and almost emotion-free. 'The Germans knew about them. They knew about Mo.'

'But this is impossible!' Beatrice insisted.

'And yet they found out,' I said. 'How could they have *known*, Beatrice?'

She thought a moment, before replying.

'The only living people who knew,' she told me, 'are standing in this garden. Other than Vincent.'

'Vincent?'

Beatrice nodded.

'So, first the Germans found out about Claude, and then my parents?' I said.

'Yes, but…'

The horror of it dawned on Beatrice's face.

'It cannot be,' she said, as I explained our conversation to Mo. The pilot nodded.

'I understand,' he said.

I turned back to Beatrice.

'It was either you or Vincent,' I said. 'And I know you did not betray us, Beatrice.'

'Dear God!' said Beatrice. 'But I arranged for him to meet some of more of our people this evening. He said he was from the south, from *Maquis* command. He knew about me and Claude, and everything we'd done.'

Mo seemed to understand.

'Vincent is your traitor, then?' he asked.

'Yes,' I replied. 'There is no one else it could be.'

Suddenly, Beatrice let out a cry.

'We must warn the others!' she told us.

'First, we bury my parents,' I said, feeling a surge of determined rage. I wondered how many other children my age had felt the same way. How many more had become older than their years.

'But we have no time,' said Beatrice.

Mo looked to me and I explained what she'd said.

'But I won't leave them like this,' I told him. 'I would rather die too.'

Mo did not reply. Instead, he went to fetch a spade.

'Where should I bury them?' he asked.

I pointed to an apple tree, in the corner of the garden.

'They planted that when I was born,' I told him. 'I will help you.'

After I'd translated, Beatrice looked towards the kitchen door.

'I will get them ready,' she said in French.

I found a smaller shovel to help Mo. We dug two holes beneath my apple tree, just deep enough to afford my parents some dignity. The cold ground was hard, and I tired very quickly, but I would not stop. Even when my arms began to cramp, I took a deep breath and carried on. When their graves were dug, Mo carried them from the house and laid them to rest. I stood and watched, shivering and wretched, my heart broken in two.

'I can finish burying them,' Mo said when he was done. 'You go inside and get warm, Joelle.'

'No,' I told him. 'I must play my part to the end.'

I often think that I should have buried something with them. A memento of some sort. Something that signified our family, our love, and our lives together. But we had no time, and I felt hollow. Besides, what good would it have done? They were gone, and nothing would bring them back.

'Hurry!' said Beatrice when we'd finished. 'Now, we must stop Vincent!'

ELEVEN

Our next concern was Mo. His appearance would make us conspicuous and easy to capture. I feared that some collaborator might see us and tell the Germans. However, I respected Mo's beliefs and knew that he would not cut his hair, nor shave. There had to be some other way.

'There is none,' Mo said eventually.

'We are wasting time,' Beatrice told us. 'We need to leave now!'

Mo glanced towards my parents' graves from the kitchen door.

'You know,' he said, 'hair will grow back. You have lost something far more precious.'

Realising what he meant, I shook my head.

'But you said that Sikhs must not cut their hair,' I reminded him.

He shook his head.

'It is an outward show of Sikhism,' he replied. 'The truth of my faith lies within my heart. Besides, we Sikhs believe in fate – we call it *kismet*.'

'*Kismet*,' I repeated.

'If our survival means that I must cut my hair, then it is meant to be. What other alternative do we have?'

Beatrice was pacing the kitchen by then, muttering under her breath. I could tell that she was scared and anxious.

'Do you have scissors and your father's shaving kit?' Mo asked.

'Yes.'

'Then fetch them, Joelle. Let us get this done and be on our way.'

I paused for a moment.

'Are you sure?' I asked.

Mo smiled and stroked his beard.

'Please,' he replied. 'Before I change my mind.'

Mo sat at the table and unwrapped his *pagri*, before unwinding his long hair.

'I would like you to cut it,' he said to me. 'It will be our pact. Our seal.'

I nodded yet part of me felt sad. The length of Mo's hair signified his faith, his absolute trust in all he believed.

'Please,' he said again.

I started slowly, cutting off small sections at a time. Meanwhile, Beatrice used another pair of scissors to shorten Mo's beard. Once it was more manageable, she used Papa's razor to shave him smooth. When we were done, Mo looked younger and even more handsome.

'Do you have a mirror?' he asked.

I handed one to him and he smiled ruefully.

'You know,' he said. 'I quite like it.'

Beatrice's impatience grew once more.

'*Mon Dieu!*' she cried. 'Do you wish to get caught?'

We packed a few belongings – food and water, a knife and some other things – and Mo dressed in some of my father's clothes and put on a peaked hat. He pulled it low over his face, then wrapped a scarf around his neck. It wasn't ideal, but it would do, and we set off. I didn't even close the door behind me. Everything I loved was gone. I no longer cared who took the rest.

That was the last time I saw our little house, on the edge of our little town, in the country of my birth. I would never return.

Our second concern was in getting across town, to the planned Resistance meeting. The Germans were on high alert and the streets might be dangerous. Beatrice told us of a few families she could trust, but I was not convinced. If Vincent knew about her contacts too, then they would be prisoners by now, or worse.

'We can go to Mrs Moreau,' I suggested. 'Leave Mo there and then run to warn your friends.'

'No,' said Mo. 'I can't let you risk yourself, Joelle.'

'I will go alone,' said Beatrice. 'You can both hide with that old witch.'

'Don't call her that!' I snapped.

'Sorry,' said Beatrice. 'I was just trying to cheer you up.'

I nodded, then smiled.

'It's fine,' I told her.

Beatrice led the way, taking every side street and alleyway she knew. We were lucky. The streets were quiet, and the Germans seemed to have gone. At least, it felt that way. I knew that they would be back soon enough. And what if we were too late to help our comrades?

'The others might have been arrested already,' I said. 'What then?'

Beatrice shrugged.

'Then, we are finished,' she whispered. 'My brother and your parents died for nothing.'

I explained our conversation to Mo, and he shook his head.

'Not for nothing,' he said with certainty. 'Their bravery and their sacrifice will not be in vain.'

We reached Mrs Moreau's bookshop and I knocked with urgency. My old friend appeared a moment later, her eyes widening with delight that did not last. Once again, I was reminded of a sickly blackbird. I burst into tears as the door opened and the blackbird began to tremble.

'My dear Joelle,' she said, taking hold of me. 'Whatever is the matter?'

'Maman and Papa are gone,' I whispered.

'Gone?' she said, eyeing both Beatrice and Mo. 'What do you mean, *gone*?'

'They were killed,' Beatrice told her. 'The Germans…'

Mrs Moreau's mouth fell open and her trembling increased. Already slight and weak, I feared the shock might kill her too.

'No!' she said. 'I refuse to believe it. This is some cruel trick…'

'It is true,' I told her. 'I am sorry.'

The old lady ushered us inside before locking the door behind us. She swore several times and then turned to Beatrice.

'Some of my neighbours called by earlier. They said that people are being arrested. Resistance people…'

'We have been betrayed,' Beatrice told her. 'Claude was also killed.'

'No!' said the old woman. 'Will these scoundrels stop at nothing? They have our country already. Must they kill our people too?'

Finally, she looked Mo up and down.

'And you?' she said. 'Are you part of this?'

I took Mrs Moreau's hand.

'We should go into the back,' I told her, wary of someone spotting us through the windows.

I led the way, past the piles of dusty books and the stuffed animals that had once seemed so comforting. With my parents gone, even those had lost their charm. In the kitchen, Mo removed the hat and scarf and Mrs Moreau gasped.

'You are an Indian!' she said. 'I met many like you during the last war.'

'Mo is a British pilot,' I explained. 'He crashed, and we hid him. The Germans are looking for him.'

She nodded.

'Can we stay here, while Beatrice warns the others?'

Mrs Moreau smiled and nodded.

'Of course, *chérie*,' she replied.

Beatrice left us then, to run her errands. Only, she did not take long. She was back within the hour, her face pale.

'They've been taken,' she told us. 'All of them…'

I translated for Mo, but he had already guessed.

'We need a new plan,' he replied. 'Can Beatrice contact Vincent?'

'Yes,' Beatrice replied for herself. 'Why?'

'I have an idea,' he replied.

TWELVE

We stayed with Mrs Moreau until darkness fell. She
made us coffee and gave us cheese and stale bread,
and I wondered how she would cope without my
parents' support. Without me. Once we left, I knew
that I would never return. That I would never see
her again.

'You seem sad, my love,' she said when she saw
my expression.

'I am,' I replied. 'I must leave here tonight, and
I cannot come back. I worry for you.'

'Pah!' she replied. 'I existed long before you
were born. I will live on once you are gone, child.'

Her reply was surprising, and my face betrayed my feelings.

'Now, now,' she added. 'Do not feel hurt, Joelle. I still love you. I will miss you with all of my heart. But please don't worry about me.'

I hugged her then and shed more tears.

'You are in the spring of your existence,' she told me. 'For me, winter has set in. Cry for your beloved parents, but not for me, *chérie*. I have lived a long and mostly happy life. Yours is only just beginning.'

'But without you, and Maman and Papa, and Beatrice and Claude, I will be left all alone. Who will I turn to when I need help or advice?'

She touched my chest, right over my heart.

'You carry us in here,' she told me. 'Trust what you know and what you believe. Be kind, be brave, be strong.'

'But…'

'Shh!' she insisted. 'Let me smell your hair for one last time. You know, I did so when you were first born?'

I nodded.

'Sweet Joelle,' she said. 'My beautiful love.'

We left an hour later, and Mrs Moreau told me not to look back. Mo sensed my pain and took my hand.

'I did not understand the words you spoke,' he told me. 'Only the emotions. But I am here for you now, Joelle. I promised your mother and I will not break that oath.'

'But you will leave for England eventually,' I replied. 'What will become of me then?'

'I will not leave without you,' he told me. 'Even if I have to take you with me.'

'To England?'

He nodded.

'Why not?' he asked. 'It is my duty to protect you now.'

Beatrice shushed us.

'We must move quickly,' she said. 'The Germans will be on our trail.'

We took an alleyway that ran beside the main square, behind my parents' bakery and on towards the north end of town. I faltered a moment, thinking about how the ovens would grow cold now, without Papa to tend to them. Had hope died too, I wondered. Had all been lost?

'The ovens?' asked Mo, as though he'd read my mind.

I nodded.

'Carry the fire within you,' he told me. 'Like my hair, the ovens are just the outward sign. The real hope lies inside you.'

We reached the street and stopped, stepping into shadows as a two-man patrol passed by. The soldiers seemed bored and lacking in focus. They did not notice the alley in which we were hiding.

'Now!' said Beatrice.

We hurried across the narrow road and down another alley. Ahead of us lay the northern part of town, and beyond that open countryside.

'The safe house is near,' Beatrice told us. 'We must be careful.'

Stopping in the shadows, we caught our breath and waited. The streets were quiet and there was no sign of the enemy.

'What shall we do when we arrive?' Beatrice asked.

'Make sure it's safe,' Mo replied. 'Any danger and we run.'

'But, Vincent?' Beatrice added. 'He must pay for betraying us.'

'We need him,' Mo told her. 'Otherwise our plan will fail.'

I kept quiet, trusting in Mo and his scheme. Five minutes later, we arrived at the safe house – a stone cottage that sat with three others on the edge of town. We checked for soldiers and for anyone watching from the cottage windows. The coast was clear. There was an outhouse, only fifteen feet from the door but well in shadow. We used it as cover. Mo went over the plan once again.

'Right,' said Beatrice in French. 'Here we go…'

She stepped from the shadows and walked quickly along the path. At the front door, she knocked three times. Mo tensed, as though he was expecting trouble.

'If anything happens,' he whispered to me, 'you stay here. Understand?'

I nodded. Vincent opened the door and looked past Beatrice.

'Where is he?' I heard him ask.

'He is heading south,' Beatrice told Vincent. 'We heard of the arrests and made a new plan.'

'But your orders were to bring him here yesterday!' Vincent told her.

He was angry.

'After what happened?' asked Beatrice. 'No – we must all run.'

'You are going after the pilot?'

Beatrice shook her head.

'No,' she said. 'I'm heading to Lille, to stay with family there. After Claude's death, I have no other choice.'

Vincent considered her words. I could almost sense his Judas brain working overtime. He was weighing things up, I was sure of it. Did he betray Beatrice, or did he run and tell his masters where Mo was going? Eventually, he nodded.

'Okay,' he replied. 'But I will stay and rebuild the Resistance here.'

Beatrice clenched her fists then, and I worried that her rage might ruin our plan. I could understand her hatred for Vincent. My own ran as deep, but we had no choice. We needed the traitor to fall for our plan. Thankfully, she soon relaxed and bid Vincent farewell. The traitorous dog shut the door on her, and she headed back our way. As she neared, she whispered.

'Does he watch from the windows?' she said in English.

'No,' Mo whispered in reply. 'He's probably already on the radio to the Germans.'

Beatrice ducked into the outhouse and I pulled the door shut. A narrow gap in the frame allowed Mo to continue watching the cottage. It took ten minutes, but eventually Vincent appeared. He picked up a bicycle and rode off, completely unaware of our proximity.

Once he was gone, we emerged.

'So, what now?' I asked.

Mo shrugged.

'Vincent will tell the Germans everything,' he said. 'They'll probably ignore Beatrice and go south. I'm much more valuable to them.'

'But if they go south, our journey becomes far more difficult,' I replied. That hadn't been part of Mo's original plan.

Mo and Beatrice smiled.

'We're going north,' said Mo.

'North?' I asked. 'But that will take us deeper into the German-controlled zone.'

'Exactly,' said Mo. 'It would be a suicide mission and completely silly. They won't suspect a thing.'

We raided the cottage for supplies and tools, filling three bags. We also borrowed coats and gloves, and Mo changed into different boots. Then we stepped back into the biting cold, ready to make our journey north.

'Are you sure about this?' I asked.

Mo had a scarf and hat around his head. I could only see his eyes, nose and mouth. He smiled.

'Don't worry, Joelle,' he said. 'I have a new plan...'

THIRTEEN

To my shame, we stole three bicycles as we left town. As we rode away, entering the Forest of Retz for cover, I wondered what Maman and Papa might have said. Ordinarily, they would have scolded me for stealing. Yet, this was no longer everyday life. This was a time of war. A time to be bold. Orphaned and on the run, I had little choice but to use what I could find. Morals and teachings about the kindness of the human heart were afterthoughts at such a time. I had to make tough decisions.

Thinking of my parents caused much pain and left me feeling glum. I said nothing as Beatrice led the way through the forest. I knew that Lille was far away, perhaps a hundred miles or more. Our journey would be slow and hazardous, even if we made it. We were travelling deeper into the German-controlled area of France. Heading towards the enemy. It made no sense, based on what I knew of the Occupation. Yet I trusted Mo, and was willing to follow him. Besides, what else was there? Without Mo and Beatrice, I was on my own.

The Forest of Retz lay north-east of Paris. It was thick with woodland and the perfect cover for us. Beatrice seemed to know every path and lane, and she refused to stop, even after two hours or so. However, even she tired eventually, and we rested.

'We go to Chauny,' she said in English. 'Then Cambrai. This route is quiet, no?'

Mo shrugged.

'I do not know your country,' he told her. 'But I trust you.'

Beatrice smiled.

'And I trust you, also,' she replied.

When I failed to speak, she glanced at me. Her expression showed sorrow.

'Dear Joelle,' she said in French. 'This is not what I wanted, but we have no choice.'

'I know.'

'I have an uncle in Cambrai, and more friends. You are welcome to live with us now. It would make me very happy.'

'You told Vincent you were going to Lille,' I replied.

'I lied,' said Beatrice. 'It was the least he deserves. I wanted to kill him.'

I nodded but said nothing more. I knew what she meant. The emptiness I felt within was Vincent's fault. He had caused this, and now he would remain free. He would not pay for his crimes. At least not at our hands. The thought depressed me further. I was not supposed to feel such things. I was not supposed to think that way. I should have been playing with Grace Deschamps, going to school, sitting beside the fire with Maman and Papa. I should have been a child.

Mo built and lit a fire. We sat around it, trying to keep warm. At some point, I fell asleep. I dreamed of my parents and our house, and the garden where I had played. I dreamed of Maman's warm embrace and Papa's ready smile. When I awoke, dawn was breaking above the treetops and I was frozen.

'Come, Joelle,' said Mo. 'We must move on.'

He removed his jacket and placed it around my shoulders.

'Wear this until you warm up,' he told me. 'I do not need it.'

Mo looked odd without his jacket, however. He still wore the hat and scarf, so most of his face and head were covered. He resembled a bandit.

'What is it?' he asked, when he caught me staring.

'Nothing,' I replied. 'I am just sad.'

He nodded and looked away, unsure of what to say, I guess.

Later that day, we emerged from the forest and travelled north-east towards the town of Chauny. The landscape opened up to reveal miles and miles of fields. Now and then, we passed small villages or hamlets, most of them deserted and often destroyed. Many of the fields lay fallow too. An eerie gloom lay over everything, a shroud of despondency and hopelessness. Was this what had become of my country, I wondered. My beautiful, vibrant country, now dazed and beaten, and bloody and worn down.

We didn't see any sign of German soldiers as we travelled. This was entirely down to luck, of course. By that evening, we were only three miles from Chauny, and my legs ached. Beatrice chose a deserted hamlet to rest in; just four houses, some outbuildings and a barn. The houses were derelict, so Mo suggested we stay in the barn. He led the way, opening the doors and ushering us inside with our bikes. Outside, the snow was returning, the flakes growing ever thicker and more frequent.

The barn was dark and damp, and cold and smelly. Yet it was welcome nonetheless. I could not have put up with another night outdoors. Not in such weather.

'I'll start a fire,' said Mo. 'Use the torches and see what you can find.'

Beatrice and I began to search. The barn was wide and long, with a second level spanning half of its area. A single wooden ladder gave access to the upper floor. I heard and smelt the tell-tale signs of rodents and other animals, and even heard a strange yelping sound. I put that down to a cat and thought nothing more of it.

'Here!' I heard Beatrice shout.

When I reached her, she was pointing at a wooden chest.

'I wonder what's inside,' she said.

She knelt and opened it, and then groaned in disappointment. The chest was empty, save for a rusting knife, a small hip flask and a moth-eaten scarf.

'I thought it might have something useful inside,' she told me.

I shrugged but did not reply. When it became clear that we would find nothing of use, we rejoined Mo and took in the fire's warming glow.

'Stay here,' he told us. 'I will check the other buildings.'

He wrapped up, took a torch and left us to stare into the flames. He had been gone perhaps twenty minutes or so when we heard the dogs barking.

'*Sacre bleu!*' Beatrice gasped. 'Germans!'

We scrambled up the ladder to the hayloft. Bales of rotting straw lay all around us.

'Climb over them,' Beatrice told me. 'To the far end.'

I thought she would follow me, but instead, she reached into her dress and removed a small revolver.

'Where did you get that?' I asked.

'It belonged to Claude,' she told me. 'Now hide, and no matter what happens, do not come out!'

'But…'

'Now, Joelle!' she urged.

I did as she asked, my heart pounding faster, dread causing chaotic thoughts. I was scared for Mo and Beatrice, but not worried about myself. I did not want to hide away, while they faced the enemy. I wanted to fight too.

I heard shouting and harsh words, but the language was French, not German. Very quickly, Beatrice spoke up, shouting to the men outside.

'We are Resistance!' she yelled. 'He is British. He cannot understand you!'

The door to the barn was kicked ajar. There stood a heavy-set man holding a shotgun. Another joined him, leading hunting dogs, and holding Mo.

'*Maquis*?' asked the man with the shotgun.

'Yes, yes!' said Beatrice. 'We were betrayed, and we ran. We are not your enemy!'

The man shrugged.

'Well, well,' he replied. 'You should have said. Welcome, my comrades!'

He lowered the gun and smiled warmly, and I closed my eyes and once more thanked our lucky stars.

FOURTEEN

Beatrice and the men spoke for a while. Mo stood with me, his shoulders tense.

'It's okay,' I told him. 'They are Resistance, like Beatrice.'

'How can we trust men we do not know?' he replied.

'Because we have no choice,' I reminded him. 'And just look at them. They are obviously on our side.'

The man with the shotgun sensed our gaze. He turned, smiled, and gestured for us to join them. When we did, he ruffled my hair.

'Beatrice tells me that you are a true hero of France,' he said. 'That your parents sacrificed themselves for our cause.'

The pain of my parents' demise must have shown on my face. The man grew sorrowful and asked my forgiveness.

'I did not mean to upset you,' he added. 'I too have lost family. A brother and an uncle, taken by these animals.'

I nodded.

'I'm sorry for your loss,' I told him.

'And I yours,' he replied. 'I am Thomas.'

He wore muddy boots, grey trousers that seemed to be made from an old sack, a thick black coat and navy cap.

'Joelle Breton,' I said.

'Please,' he said. 'We meant no harm. You are all welcome here.'

He nodded towards Mo.

'And you,' he said in heavily accented English, 'you are pilot for the British?'

'Yes,' said Mo. 'I am trying to get back to England.'

Thomas raised an eyebrow.

'But you head north?' he said. 'That is not good. Too many Germans.'

Mo shrugged and said nothing, and Thomas changed the subject.

'Hungry?'

We nodded.

'We have rabbit stew and bread. Come!'

Thomas led us past the first three derelict houses and through the door of the fourth. The ground floor was uninhabitable – open to the elements and freezing. Thomas went to the rear, where junk lay piled up. He pulled aside old wooden crates and sacks of woodchips until I saw a secret hatch.

'A cellar,' I said, as I remembered my old house.

'Our hideaway,' said Thomas.

His friend left the dogs to roam the upper floors, before joining us with Beatrice.

'This is Jean,' Beatrice told us.

He was younger than Thomas but of the same build – stocky and powerful, with wide shoulders.

'He is my son,' Thomas confirmed.

Just inside the hatch, an oil lantern hung from the stone wall. Thomas lit it and led the way. I was expecting a narrow, damp space, but the cellar was deep and wide and cosy.

'We widened and reinforced it,' Thomas explained. 'It is linked to the ones beneath the other houses.'

'We have several escape hatches around the hamlet too,' Jean added.

'It is a warren!' Beatrice exclaimed. 'A perfect hideaway.'

Thomas gave a proud smile.

'When the Germans invaded, we decided to dig in,' he explained. 'We are active in the Resistance too.'

I glanced at Mo, who seemed uninterested. He hadn't relaxed at all.

'What's the matter?' I whispered.

'Nothing,' he replied. 'I am simply being careful.'

I nodded and left him alone. After our betrayal at Vincent's hands, Mo's reluctance was no surprise. I wondered whether I was too trusting of Thomas and Jean. Should I have been as wary as Mo, perhaps?

'Sit, sit!' said Thomas, clapping his hand across Mo's back. 'We eat, then we talk!'

We ate and chatted and shared stories of our time under the Germans. Thomas and Beatrice then left us to discuss Resistance matters and Jean went to check on his dogs. I turned to Mo, who seemed more relaxed than earlier.

'What you said?' I began. 'Was it true?'

'What do you mean?' he asked.

'When you said you'd take me with you?'

Mo's offer had been playing on my mind since we'd left my home. Left Mrs Moreau and the bakery, and the buried remains of my dear parents. I was all alone, except for Mo and Beatrice, and I knew that a choice was coming. Soon, I would have to decide whether to remain with Beatrice or to follow Mo. My head told me to stay, but my heart had other plans. Yet, that longing to leave France seemed silly and ill-judged. I hardly knew Mo and life in a foreign country seemed unimaginable.

'Sikhs live by a moral code,' Mo told me. 'Part of which is to remain true to our oaths. I have given you my word, Joelle. I will not let you down.'

'But I am not your family,' I replied. 'You have no duty to me.'

Mo shook his head.

'We are all family,' he said. 'Every man, woman and child on this Earth. I believe that all of creation is one whole. We are bound together, each of us, by invisible links, and all are equally important.'

'But…'

'The decision is yours to make,' he told me. 'If you trust in my care, I will always look after you. If you choose to remain in your own country, that I will also accept.'

'And this is what Sikhism teaches you?' I wondered aloud.

Mo shrugged.

'Perhaps,' he replied. 'But life teaches me this too. Fate brought us together, Joelle, and gave me a duty. I accept it with gratitude.'

'What will people think of a French girl and an Indian man travelling together?' I asked.

'They will think whatever they choose,' he said. 'It is of no consequence.'

'But what of the details?' I added. 'Where to live and school, and such things…'

'One step at a time,' he told me. 'There is no other way. These are unusual times, and we are victims of circumstance.'

Neither of us spoke again until Beatrice returned, a smile across her face.

'Thomas has promised us transport,' she explained. 'A small truck to get us towards Lille.'

I frowned.

'Won't that make us conspicuous?' I asked.

'Perhaps,' she replied. 'But our journey will be faster. Besides, we can take country lanes and steer clear of German patrols.'

I wasn't so sure, and Mo said nothing. Beatrice smiled again.

'Get some rest,' she told us. 'We leave before dawn.'

We bid Thomas and Jean goodbye in the darkness, setting off towards the north once more. The vehicle was an old farm truck, with a flat bed and crude suspension that jolted our bones as we trundled over rutted tracks. Thomas had given us a rifle and ammunition, and food for the journey. As light broke, we were well advanced, and Beatrice seemed to enjoy the drive. She'd handed me a crudely drawn map, with various towns and cities pinpointed in pencil – Chauny and Cambrai, Lens and Lille. Written below was a warning to avoid any major roads.

'The Germans will not patrol the country lanes,' Beatrice repeated from the previous evening. 'At least, that is my hope…'

'And if they do spot us?' I asked.

'Then we fight,' said Beatrice, her face set.

I explained what had been said to Mo, and he nodded.

'We have no choice,' he said. 'We go where fate takes us.'

Fate seemed to smile on us too. We made great progress and soon passed Chauny, the first of our markers. Bar some well-meaning locals, we saw no one and sensed no danger. It was almost pleasurable, like a scenic drive towards a summer vacation spot.

But it did not last…

FIFTEEN

'GERMANS!'

I awoke with a start, having dozed off earlier. Beatrice swore and swerved from the road, between some trees. I hung on as the truck shuddered to a halt, using my arms to brace myself.

'What now?' Beatrice asked in English.

'They will have seen us,' he replied. 'We need to get out and hide.'

I was still dazed and stumbled out behind Mo, who had grabbed Thomas's rifle and some ammunition.

'I fell asleep,' I told him. 'Where are they?'

'About a quarter of a mile away,' said Mo. 'A roadblock with two jeeps. Three or four men at most.'

Beatrice pointed to the road.

'Wait here,' she said.

I watched her edge towards the treeline, right where we'd left the road. She crouched by an oak tree and peered towards the roadblock. Suddenly, she turned and sprinted back to us.

'They come!' she shouted. 'Quick!'

Mo took my hand and pulled me away, into a thicket. I was immediately reminded of our first meeting. Already, it felt like a lifetime ago. We pushed through the bushes, Beatrice right behind us.

'Hurry!' she called.

Only, we were almost past the thicket. Any further and there would be no cover for us. Beatrice drew her pistol and tapped Mo on the shoulder.

'We fight?' she asked.

Mo glanced my way, his eyes full of resignation and sadness.

'You must hide here,' he told me. 'Do not come out; do not watch what happens. And cover your ears, Joelle. This is not for you.'

I wanted to protest. To say I was not a child. But that is exactly what I was in that moment. A scared child faced with yet more loss.

'Don't fight,' I begged them. 'You will be killed, and I will be left alone.'

'We must,' Mo insisted. 'If they find us, they will not spare us. You know this.'

'But…'

Mo embraced me for a moment.

'Please, Joelle,' he said.

I nodded, wiped away tears and did as he asked. Beatrice kept low, the pistol ready, and went to the left, deeper into the trees. Mo went right, using the rifle to push past thick undergrowth until he was hidden. I heard German voices and then two of the soldiers appeared in the clearing between my hiding place and the treeline protecting Beatrice. Each held a rifle at shoulder height as they scanned the area.

I closed my eyes and covered my ears, but not for very long. Curiosity is a strange thing – so intrinsic to our being as humans that even fear can be overcome. I simply could not ignore what was happening, much as I might regret it afterwards.

Only, I had grown immune to such things since my parents' death, or so I thought at the time.

I opened my eyes and uncovered my ears in time to hear the first shot from Beatrice's pistol. One of the soldiers screamed and fell, and then the other began to fire wildly. His shots were aimless, ripping into tree trunks but finding no foe. With his concentration on Beatrice's position, he did not sense Mo, who also fired. More screams and then Beatrice appeared and finished the job, and my stomach grew tight and swirled with knots.

'GO!' she called, as more Germans entered the fray.

Mo was already in hiding, and I watched Beatrice sprint around to flank the newcomers. She was not stealthy enough and the soldiers spotted her. They began to fire too, and Beatrice yelped and then fell into the undergrowth. I screamed then, giving away my position, and the soldiers turned to me. I watched in horror as they raised their rifles, ready to fire indiscriminately.

Suddenly, Mo appeared behind them. He aimed and fired, and the lead soldier fell. The other turned too slowly and Mo's aim was true once more. With both men down, he rushed towards me, diving into the thicket.

'Hurry!' he gasped. 'We must get back to the road.'

'Beatrice!' I screamed.

I pointed to where she had fallen and led Mo towards her.

'She was hit,' I told him. 'I am sure of it.'

Mo slung the rifle over his shoulder, and we hurried to find her. But as we entered the treeline on the far side of the clearing, Beatrice stood up.

'I'm okay,' she said in French, before switching to English. 'Good, good!'

I rushed to embrace her.

'I thought they had killed you!'

Beatrice shook her head.

'No, no,' she insisted. 'I slipped and fell. There was a rabbit hole. My ankle is sprained.'

The three of us turned back towards the road. Beatrice was hobbling, each step causing her to grimace. We made slow progress, but it did not matter now that the soldiers were dead.

'What shall we do?' I asked Mo.

'We push on,' he said. 'Once the patrol is missed, the Germans will flood the area. We need to be far away when that happens.'

'I did not obey you,' I admitted. 'I saw everything.'

Mo considered me for a moment before replying.

'Then,' he said, 'we will deal with that later. For now, we must move on.'

I nodded before helping Beatrice back into our truck. She reversed on to the road and we continued on our way. At the roadblock, Mo scavenged what he could from the two jeeps and destroyed the radio. He found a bag of sweets, which he shared with me, and canisters of water that were even more welcome.

'Let's go,' he said. 'There is no time to lose.'

Behind us lay four dead human beings. And yet I did not feel a thing. It was just another incident. Something else to be endured. There was no horror, no sadness, no feelings of disgust. Just the cold and harsh reality of war. In that respect, my heart had grown as hard as the roads along which we travelled.

SIXTEEN

The remaining miles to Cambrai passed without incident. No one came after us. The further north-east we travelled, the bleaker the landscape became. The smallest villages and hamlets were deserted, and crops lay rotting in the fields, as though we were passing through some dystopian nightmare. A landscape inspired by darkness and destruction, leeched clean of warmth and joy and love and life. Only the major towns were busy, and those we avoided, in order to bypass German patrols.

As dusk gave way to darkness, we arrived at a small town called Bourlon, to the west of Cambrai. There, Beatrice stopped at a farmhouse and a stout man resembling her brother Claude came out to greet us. He was older than Claude had been, with white whiskers and hair, and a rugged and pitted complexion compounded by a bulbous and seemingly scarlet nose.

'Beatrice, *chérie*!' the man exclaimed, as he hugged his niece.

'Uncle!' Beatrice sobbed, unable to control her emotions.

Their embrace continued for some moments before Beatrice finally extricated herself and gestured towards us.

'My friends,' she said in French. 'Joelle Breton and Mohinder Singh.'

Beatrice's uncle nodded and beckoned us. He did not even give Mo a second glance. As though Indians were common in his world.

'Come, come!' he said. 'Eat and rest!'

Mo followed my lead and we entered a warm and inviting house that reeked of roasted garlic and coffee, warm bread and crackling logs. I felt like I had entered heaven, so welcome were those homely aromas.

'We are safe here,' Beatrice told me. 'Rest and then we will discuss your future.'

I thanked her and turned to Mo.

'I need to sleep,' I told him.

'Me too,' he replied.

His brown skin was grey with dirt and his eyes weary, and his relief at this respite was obvious. I felt the same way, but there was still something playing on my mind.

'Tell me of your plan,' I said.

Mo shrugged.

'That can wait,' he replied.

'But…'

'Joelle,' he said in his melodic accent, and I relented.

Beatrice showed us to a room towards the rear, where two sparsely furnished beds lay against opposing walls.

'Sleep now,' she told me.

'Thank you,' I replied. 'For everything.'

Fully rested and almost refreshed, we made our goodbyes the following morning. I had risen at dawn, my head a maelstrom of indecisive thoughts. What would be my decision? Where would I go? What would become of me, either way? I sat on a garden bench, looking out across the frozen farmyard. The cold bit deep but I tried to ignore it. Besides, it focused my mind. I did not hear Mo until he spoke from behind me.

'Joelle?'

I turned, smiled and made room on the bench.

'It is not easy,' I said unnecessarily. 'I can't seem to settle on one thing. Each time I think I've decided, another doubt creeps in.'

'Tell me,' said Mo, taking the space beside me.

'France is my country,' I told him. 'It is my home. But since Maman and Papa, it feels colder. I think of them constantly. I am reminded of them constantly. Every lane and every field. Every smell and every taste. So, a new beginning makes sense.'

Mo nodded.

'But?' he asked.

'But England seems so foreign,' I admitted. 'And I worry that I would become a burden to you, or to someone else. How would I survive and live?'

'You are not a burden,' he replied. 'Not for me, nor Beatrice, nor anyone. Never think of yourself that way.'

'But what happens if you return to India?' I added. 'What would I do then?'

Mo shrugged.

'I have been wondering the same thing,' he said. 'However, I do not wish to return. I like England and hope to make it my home. Even if I did have to go, I would happily take you with me.'

'To India?'

'If need be,' he replied.

'But I know nothing of India,' I told him. 'And your family – would they accept some French girl?'

'I do not care,' Mo said. 'However, I know that leaving you here, with Beatrice and her family, will be fine. It is probably the best course to take.'

'You want to leave me here?'

My tone was emotional and laced with surprise. Mo realised and swiftly shook his head.

'No,' he said. 'I accept your decision, whatever that may be. If you do not wish to stay, I will not force you.'

'And when we find difficulties in England?' I asked.

'We will overcome them,' he replied. 'You have my word, Joelle. My most solemn promise, on everything that I hold sacred.'

'But the English may not let me stay,' I said.

'They will not send you back here,' he replied. 'That would be heartless and cruel. There is a war on and there will be many refugees. You will simply become one of thousands.'

I considered his words until Beatrice appeared with tin cups of coffee and a warm smile.

'So?' she said in French. 'What will you do, *chérie*?'

I looked up at her and smiled in return.

'I will go to England,' I told her.

She nodded and held out my cup of coffee.

'Perhaps that is best,' she said, her tone tainted with sorrow. 'I wish it were not so, of course. Yet I imagine being here without your parents will be hard.'

'You are correct,' I said. 'But I cannot thank you enough, for all that you have done. I only wish we could go back to before the war.'

'Me too,' she replied. 'That's the thing about life, Joelle. We can never go back. The past shapes us. It makes us who we are. It cannot be undone. All we have is what we make of tomorrow.'

I thought on her words for a while.

'I will return one day,' I promised. 'Perhaps I will find you here?'

Beatrice shrugged. Her nose was bright pink with cold.

'Maybe,' she said. 'I would like that.'

SEVENTEEN

Later, when Mo finally revealed his plan, he sounded completely insane. Beatrice translated for her uncle, Georges, who simply shook his huge, weathered head.

'It is suicide!' he gruffly exclaimed in French. 'Have you lost your mind?'

Mo seemed to get the point, despite the language difficulties. We were sitting around a battered kitchen table, after a breakfast of bread and jam. Mo cleared his throat.

'I know it sounds crazy,' he told us. 'But there is no other way. Besides, the Germans are looking for enemies on the ground, not in the skies.'

'But, to steal a *German* plane?' I asked. 'From a *German* airbase? We'll be killed.'

Mo shook his head. He seemed fresher that morning, and far happier. His smile had returned alongside the sparkle in his eyes. Perhaps it was the thought of escaping from France, or maybe the thrill of his plan. Only, his plan made me question his sanity.

'The Germans raid mostly at night,' Mo continued. 'They use the darkness as cover, to avoid detection. But they won't send all of their planes at once. So, we simply sneak on to an airfield, hide until a night raid begins and steal one of the spare planes.'

'Absolutely out of the question!' said Beatrice. 'I cannot believe this is your plan!'

She translated again, and this time Uncle Georges walked off muttering to himself.

'It will work!' Mo insisted. 'That's the point. It's so dangerous, they would never even consider it. And we'll be away before they find out.'

Beatrice munched on a piece of bread and did not reply.

'If we do try this,' I said, 'where is the nearest airfield?'

'I don't know,' Mo admitted. 'I was hoping Beatrice's family could help.'

Beatrice finished her mouthful and sighed.

'I will ask my uncle,' she told us. 'But he is more likely to slap you than help you. And he has big hands.'

As Beatrice left, I caught Mo smiling.

'Really?' I asked. 'This is actually your plan?'

He nodded.

'I thought of it at your friend's bookshop,' he told me.

'Mrs Moreau?'

'Yes,' he said. 'I saw a book about planes on a side table. It won't be easy, Joelle, but we can try.'

'Well,' I said with a grin. 'We've got nothing to lose. Except our lives…'

'Have you ever flown in a plane before?' Mo asked.

'Never,' I said.

'It is a wonderful experience,' he told me. 'The freedom, the rush of air, the sense of absolute calm…'

'I must be as insane as you,' I told him. 'You're making it sound like some wonderful adventure.'

'You like my plan?'

I grinned again.

'I want to fly,' I told him. 'So, yes.'

Uncle Georges remained unimpressed but thanks to Beatrice's insistence, he decided to help us. He disappeared for a few hours, leaving us the afternoon to get some rest. If Mo's plan worked, it would be a very long night.

Georges returned at dusk, with an old lady driving a single-horse cart. The bed was packed with hay and it stank.

'What is this?' I asked Georges.

'Transport,' he replied. 'If you insist on getting killed, this will take you to your doom, child.'

'But it stinks!' I complained.

'Pah!' hissed the old woman. 'Listen to this princess! It is simply horse muck. Nothing to fear!'

The woman was barely five feet tall. Her dark eyes were beady, and grey whiskers sprouted from her chin. She was wrapped up in a crocheted black shawl and smoking a pipe. A swallow tattoo was etched upon her left hand, and I found myself warming to her, despite her manner.

'I'm no princess,' I told her.

'I can see that,' she replied. 'You're covered in dirt and your hair looks worse than my straw. What prince would have you?'

'Perhaps those whom you've yet to turn into frogs, witch?' I snapped.

Her eyes narrowed, and I thought I'd gone too far, but then she cackled and coughed and slapped Georges' shoulder.

'I like this one,' she told him. 'Pity she's about to be killed by those German dogs.'

She winked at me.

'Don't worry,' she added. 'I'll give you a decent burial, princess.'

I grinned again.

'If you live that long,' I countered.

Beatrice fetched Mo from inside and when he saw the cart, he nodded.

'We hide in the straw?' he asked Beatrice.

'That is the idea,' she replied. 'If you're still doing it.'

'Yes,' he said, eyeing the old woman.

'What is this?' she asked Georges.

'Indian,' Georges replied. 'A pilot for the British.'

'He is handsome,' she said, winking at me. 'Like the ones that came during the last war. Only they had beards and wore cloth upon their heads.'

I translated, and Mo burst into laughter.

'Tell her I follow in the footsteps of my countrymen,' he said.

On understanding, the woman smiled.

'I served many of them coffee,' she replied. 'They were brave souls. I am honoured to help him. Even if he is going to die.'

This banter continued via my translations, until finally Beatrice put an end to it.

'We have much to do,' she told us. 'Come inside!'

Mo took my arm.

'You can change your mind at any time,' he told me. 'I will not think badly of you, Joelle. This will be a dangerous mission.'

'I won't change my mind,' I replied. 'I go with you, come what may. Maman told me to be brave. I will honour her words.'

'Then enjoy your last hours in France,' he told me. 'We will breakfast in England.'

And that was my last memory of France. Hidden beneath piles of stinking straw, with only Mo and dung beetles for company, as the cart trundled along frozen lanes, towards the nearest airfield.

'No one will stop an old lady!' the woman shouted, as much for herself as us. 'They do not see me and my horse as a threat.'

She wittered on for the entire journey, perhaps an hour or more. Finally, the cart came to a stop. I heard the old woman dismount and pet her grey and aging horse, before she came around and uncovered us. I brushed the remnants of horse manure and straw from my hair. God only knows how much I stank. I had not bathed in days, and this was a final insult to hygiene.

We had stopped by a copse of trees, next to a dilapidated barn that sat alone, the accompanying farmhouse long gone.

'You walk from here,' the woman said to me. 'Any closer, and I risk alarming the Germans.'

'Thank you for your courage,' I told her.

'Courage?' she spat. 'This isn't courage. You should have heard my husband farting. I survived fifty years of it. *That* was courage!'

I did not know whether to laugh or cry. The old woman was shockingly unguarded in her words, but she also had real warmth. Yet I was leaving my country, perhaps even to die in the attempt. My emotions were a mess.

'Take heart, dear girl,' the woman whispered. 'You are the courageous one, for sure. I hope you can trick these German dogs and live a long and peaceful life.'

'And if I die?'

The woman grinned.

'Then I will drink a toast to your stupidity,' she joked.

'And choke on the last drop,' I told her.

We embraced and then she remounted her cart and left us alone. As I explained our conversation to Mo, he seemed preoccupied.

'What is it?' I asked.

He pointed across a field to our left. In the middle distance, I spotted lights and heard the unmistakeable sound of engines running.

'The airfield,' he said. 'They are readying for a night raid. We don't have much time.'

EIGHTEEN

Darkness provided all the cover that we required. Mo had assumed that the Germans would be too busy preparing their planes to worry about intruders. He was correct. That was what made his plan so ingenious. Gaining entry to a German-controlled airbase was incredibly perilous. And the Germans did not believe that anyone could be that reckless. And yet here we were, hurrying across a frozen field, with only the lights ahead to guide us. Later I would learn of an English phrase that perfectly explained our mission that night. We were fools, rushing in where angels feared to tread.

At the perimeter, we found a ramshackle fence through which we passed with ease. Our enemies were so arrogant that they had not even strengthened their defences. It worked right into our hands. Once on the airfield, we slowed down, and looked for cover. A stack of wooden crates became our first hiding place. From about a hundred yards, we watched the Germans rushing around, the pilots shouting orders to the ground staff.

'Listen out for guard dogs,' Mo whispered. 'If they sense us, we're doomed.'

'Okay,' I replied.

We waited for some time, and adrenaline and fear coursed through my veins. I wanted to shout and scream but held that urge. My left leg began to tremble, and my heart thumped inside my chest.

'Are you scared?' I whispered.

Mo nodded.

'Fear is our friend,' he replied. 'It will focus our minds.'

'How long do we wait?'

Mo pointed towards the planes, and I heard the engines firing up again. The ground staff began to retreat, and the first plane edged away, rolling towards the runway.

'We must wait until all are airborne,' said Mo. 'It won't be long now.'

One by one, the planes began to leave. Mo recognised them as Messerschmitt Bf 109s. They were grey, with black crosses outlined in white painted on the side and wings, and the Nazi swastika on the tail.

'They will not fly very far,' he told me. 'But they are deadly in the air.'

I counted seven planes taking off at first, and then three more immediately afterwards.

'Damn!' I heard Mo exclaim, as my own heart sank.

Far from leaving unoccupied planes behind, the Germans had launched every single one. Mo's plan was ruined.

'This is not good,' he whispered. 'Let's see what the ground crew do next.'

The remaining men began to walk back towards an aerodrome about a quarter of a mile further back. They carried lamps and torches with them, although the lights around the runaway remained lit. As their voices receded, Mo told me to wait.

'I will take a look around,' he said.

I shook my head.

'No,' I insisted. 'That was not the deal. We go together.'

'But Joelle…' he began, only for me to insist once more.

'If something happens to you,' I told him, 'I will be stuck out here alone. We live together, or we die together.'

He relented and told me to follow close behind.

'In my exact footsteps,' he said. 'And if they see us, you run back to the fence, understand?'

I nodded.

'You don't look back, you don't wait for me, you just run.'

'Yes,' I replied.

My resolve hardened once again. The thought of my dead parents gave me greater courage. I would not die running from the monsters who had murdered those I loved. If they wanted to kill me, they would have to look me in the eyes.

Mo set off at a brisk pace, and I ran to keep up. To the left of the aerodrome were two single-storey huts, each about thirty feet long. To the right were more crates, and tanks of fuel. Mo slowed down as we skirted the landing lights, sticking to the shadows. Very quickly we closed in on the aerodrome.

'Wait,' he whispered.

He crouched and I followed suit. We were to the right, opposite the fuel drums and crates.

'There!' he whispered excitedly.

At first, I could not see what had animated him, but then I spotted it. Another plane, although very different to the Bf 109s. It had two sets of wings, one above the other, and two cockpits. It was the same light grey colour, with the same markings, but looked almost comical where the Bf 109s were sleek and deadly.

'Is that a good plane?' I asked.

Mo shook his head.

'It's a biplane,' he told me. 'Old-fashioned. They probably use it to train pilots. I think it may be a Bücker Bü 131 but I can't be sure...'

'So, we're stuck?' I said.

'No,' Mo told me. 'With enough fuel, it will get us back to England.'

'It will?'

Mo nodded.

'As long as we don't come across any British planes,' he added.

'Why?' I asked, before realising my error. 'Oh…'

The plane had German markings. If the British saw it, they would attack, and we would be shot down. But that might happen regardless of which German plane we stole.

'It's our only hope now,' said Mo. 'Quick!'

He sprinted towards the fuel drums, and I kept pace. We ducked behind them just in time. Two Germans appeared from a side door of the aerodrome. They stood by some smaller wooden crates, and one of them picked up some matches to light their cigarettes. They stood for five minutes, chatting and laughing, before going back inside.

'This time you wait,' said Mo, pulling a length of rubber tube from a drum. 'I will check the fuel.'

The Bücker Bü 131 was nearly twenty feet long with wings that were slightly wider. It looked even more comical close up, but what did I know? Mo was the pilot, and he seemed convinced of its worth. Who was I to question him? Instead, I kept an eye on the door, praying that more Germans didn't appear. When Mo returned, he smelt of petrol. He gave me a thumbs up and smiled.

'It's good,' he told me. 'They must keep it ready to fly.'

'How did you check the fuel level?' I asked.

'The rubber tube,' he explained. 'You push it into the tank and suck until the fuel hits yours lips. The quicker the fuel appears, the fuller the tank.'

'That's why you reek of it?'

Mo smiled.

'What's the harm in another odour now?' he asked. 'We smell like farm animals already.'

'Won't the Germans hear the engine starting?'

'Yes, they will,' he said. 'But I've got a plan for that as well.'

'What will you do?'

Mo told me to get into the rear cockpit of the plane and wait.

'But...'

'Just listen,' he insisted. 'Please, Joelle! You'll find goggles and a flight jacket. Put them on. There's a helmet too. We'll be flying low, but it will get very cold up there.'

'How cold?'

'Just do it!' he snapped.

Annoyed, I trudged over to the plane and used a wooden step to clamber into the cockpit. Close up, I could see that the wings were made of wood and fabric, while the body was metal of some sort. The cockpit was small, with a single seat, but big enough for me. As I put on the goggles, jacket and helmet – all way too big for me – I watched Mo. He pushed a fuel drum over and the viscous liquid began to slop on to the ground. Then he slowly heaved the drum towards the plane, leaving a trail of fuel. Just before he reached me, he let the drum go and ran over to where the Germans had been smoking. The matches were still on the crates, and he grabbed the entire box.

He sprinted back to the plane and clambered aboard, and put on his own jacket, goggles and hat.

'Hold tight,' he told me. 'Things are about to get a little hot.'

He took several matches, struck them, and dropped them to the ground. Instantly, the fuel took light. Grinning, he threw the whole box into the flames.

'Time to go!' he shouted, gunning the engine.

The plane exploded into life. It sounded like a bomb on ignition, and very quickly, he was steering us away from the aerodrome and towards freedom. Behind us, the Germans came running, but suddenly a real explosion rocked the earth beneath us. There were nine or ten fuel drums in the path of Mo's flames and half them had exploded. The rest went up in ones and twos, and suddenly everything around them was ablaze. A siren began to howl and then the gunshots started.

'Hold on!' Mo yelled above the din.

He gunned the throttle and soon we were racing away from the aerodrome. And then, without any warning, the plane's nose tilted skywards, and we were climbing into the air. My stomach somersaulted and I felt sick, as a gust of wind buffeted the plane. The ground beneath us zinged with gunfire, and then the bullets whooshed past us.

'JUST A FEW MORE SECONDS!' Mo shouted.

'WHAT?'

His reply was lost in the rush of air and turbulence and engine noise. The wings rattled and the plane's body creaked. A bullet hit the rear, inches from where I sat. A second one whizzed past my head. I closed my eyes and began to pray.

NINETEEN

When I opened my eyes, we had escaped the airfield and were flying high above open countryside. Here and there I could see faint lights, but little else on the ground. It was just a mass of black. Above us were dark grey clouds and the wind buffeted us all the way, blasting my face and making breathing difficult at times.

'HOW LONG WILL IT TAKE?' I yelled, but my words were instantly lost. The noise from the propellers and engines, and the wind, made conversation impossible.

Mo turned his head and gave me a thumbs-up sign, which I reciprocated. Then, with little else to do, I sat back and tried to make out what was below us. It took a while for my eyes to adjust, but there was not much to see. In front of me were several dials, none of which made any sense except for the compass. This showed that we were flying north-west, at a steady angle. I assumed that Mo knew which way to go but wondered how he would know for sure in the darkness.

The wings creaked and groaned once again, and then I heard a slight ripping sound. Alarmed, I considered tapping Mo on the shoulder, but didn't. He must have heard it too, and it didn't seem to bother him.

Suddenly, Mo changed direction, to our left and upwards, and my stomach flipped over and the breath caught in my throat. The move left me shaken, and I wondered why he'd made it, until I heard the roar of faster and more mobile planes. Mo gestured below and I peered into the night, but despite the new engine noise, I could not see any planes. Three of them must have passed close to us, and then all was normal once again.

Mo lowered our altitude, re-setting our direction by the compass. We were flying due north now, with just a slight western variation after a few minutes. I longed to ask him about flying the plane, but there was little point. Instead, I thought of Maman and Papa. They had talked of flying as a great dream to be fulfilled someday. Here I was, living their dreams for them, as they lay buried under the soil of our beautiful country.

I began to cry then, sobbing uncontrollably and without embarrassment. Up there, amongst the dark clouds, no one could hear my wailing, and no one could judge my tears. Every emotion I'd held since that awful day exploded, until there was nothing left inside me. My eyes stung and my throat grew hoarse, but a great burden had been lifted. I was not free of sorrow, of course. That would never truly leave me. But I did feel better, and that was worth a great deal.

Soon, I closed my eyes again and began to drift off, my head lolling, until everything faded away...

An abrupt rush of turbulence snapped me from my dreams. The plane was tilting to the right and Mo seemed to be struggling. I had no idea how long I'd been asleep, nor where we were. I felt dazed, still half asleep, and unable to think properly. Below, there was only darkness and nothing in the skies all around us. I wondered how far we had come, and how close England was.

The plane lolled sideways again, and then it began to descend rapidly. My insides churned and I thought that I might vomit, but finally Mo managed to rectify the problem. He turned to me and smiled. I could not smile in return. He gestured below and shouted something. I gestured to my ears and shook my head. He tried again, and this time I understood.

'ENGLAND!'

My eyes widened. I pointed downwards and nodded. Mo nodded in return. Had I slept for the entire journey, I wondered. Or had it been *that* fast?

A sudden blast rocked the plane. It veered leftwards and sank at pace, and I screamed. Mo spun around and began struggling with the controls once more. Another blast exploded to my right and I saw a cloud of smoke. I had no idea what was being fired at us. I only knew that we were under attack.

Mo managed to wrestle control, but now he was taking evasive action. The plane shuddered and screeched, and I feared that it might break in half.

The metal beneath my feet flexed and squealed. He turned to the right, then left, then right again. The plane was rigid and did not respond quickly. And the projectiles continued to rain in.

Mo tried to bring the nose up, to take us higher and away from the missiles, but it would not respond…

And then, just as my head cracked against the instrument cluster, the engine died, and I fell unconscious…

When I came to, I was being carried on a man's shoulders. I struggled to move but my left arm was broken. The pain caused me to vomit.

'MO!' I screamed through the pain.

The man did not reply, and then I heard more people. English people. They had gathered by a farmhouse, and when I was laid down, a woman's kindly face appeared above me. She had blonde hair and pale blue eyes. She smiled warmly.

'Stay calm, young lady,' she said. 'You're safe now.'

She cleaned my face with a damp rag and stayed until a medic arrived. He was old and gruff in appearance, but he smiled too.

'You're very lucky,' he told me. 'Only a broken arm. We'll have you fixed up in no time.'

'My friend…?' I croaked. 'Mo?'

'The pilot?' asked the kindly woman.

'Yes…'

'He's in the wreckage. The military police will get him. Dirty Nazi…'

I shook my head.

'No!' I said. 'He is British. Mohinder Singh, RAF. We escaped!'

The two of them looked puzzled.

'RAF?'

'YES!' I said, wincing in pain. 'Please, help him!'

The woman turned and approached another man, this one in a dark uniform, and began to point. I assumed she was gesturing towards the crashed plane. I couldn't hear her words, but she seemed insistent. The uniformed man nodded and took off at pace. The woman returned to me.

'Don't worry,' she told me. 'I told them about your friend.'

The medic filled a syringe and injected my good arm.

'Morphine,' he explained. 'Just close your eyes and the pain will soon be gone.'

I did as he asked and prayed that Mo would survive. I wanted to get up and help him, but the drug coursing through my veins prevented it. Instead, I passed out once again.

I did not see Mo again for nearly a week. His condition was critical and he had been moved to a military hospital. I remained behind and stayed with a local family. The Warrens were generous and warm-hearted, but I spent my time worrying about Mo. Praying that he would survive his injuries. I had nothing save for the clothes I wore, and was given no updates as to Mo's chances of survival. I could not sleep and had little appetite for sustenance or cheer.

Our time together, however brief, had brought us as close as father and daughter. Our bond of love and trust, and mutual support, was solid. My parents were gone forever. I had left Beatrice behind, and felt as though I'd abandoned poor Mrs Moreau. My best friend had been taken, my home and my country were lost to me. All that remained were memories of a life no longer lived, and Mo. I could not bear to lose him too.

So, on that morning I was taken to see him, my gloom lifted. Miraculously, he had survived. The nurse explained that he would soon be well enough to leave.

'He might walk with a limp,' she added. 'But he's been very lucky. And brave too.'

She glanced at my broken arm.

'You as well, by the look of it.' Her smile was full of kindness and cheer.

As I sat watching Mo sleep, I wondered what fate would bring. Would we be allowed to remain together? Would Mo stay in England and stay with me? It was a strange feeling – both hopeful and frightening at once. Yet despite my fears and recurrent melancholy, I began to dream of making a new home somewhere. For the first time since my parents had died, a brighter future seemed possible. A tiny sliver of light entered my heart, a little piece of hope renewed.

Smiling, I took hold of Mo's hand and thought of Maman and Papa in brighter, happier times.

EPILOGUE

When she was finished, Joelle wiped away a single tear. She took hold of my hand and gave it a squeeze.

'I must leave,' she told me. 'It's a long way back to Scotland.'

'No!' I replied. 'You have to stay. Please, you need to meet my mum. And what about your story? People should hear it.'

Joelle shook her head.

'It was *our* story,' she said sadly. 'It belonged to Mo and me. Now he is gone, and I have no wish to tell it again.'

'But someone should write it down,' I insisted. 'Like at school, we learn about World War Two, but no one ever tells us about people like my great-grandfather.'

'Then you write it down,' she replied. '*You* tell our story.'

'But I've got so many questions,' I told her. 'What happened after my great-grandfather left hospital and where did you go?'

Joelle stood and took an iPhone from her pocket.

'My granddaughter taught me to use this,' she said. 'There's an app for taxis. Mine has arrived…'

'But…?'

Joelle took my hand.

'Walk with me,' she said.

We strolled down to the main road, where her cab stood waiting.

'The only thing you need to know is that Mo saved me and looked after me,' Joelle said. 'He was the kindest and most noble human being I have ever known. What he did for me was so selfless, so brave, that I feel humbled still. That is all that matters, Simpreet. The rest isn't important. Just make it up.'

I asked her for her contact information, but she shook her head.

'I live just north of Loch Ness,' she told me. 'If you're ever up that way, find me. There aren't many Joelle Bretons where I live. Besides, when you go through Mo's things, you'll find my address on the letters. Write to me. I'd like that.'

'So, you're leaving?' I asked. 'Just like that?'

Joelle nodded.

'I've been leaving my entire life,' she replied. 'It's what I do best.'